WALKING
ON
THE
MOON

SIX STORIES AND
A NOVELLA

BARBARA WILSON

The Seal Press *Seattle*

Acknowledgements

"Il Circo delle Donne" previously appeared in *Maenad;* "The Hulk" in *Common Lives, Lesbian Lives.*

My thanks to Faith Conlon and Hylah Jacques for editorial help with successive versions of several stories, to Rachel da Silva and John D. Berry for production and copy-editing and to Edith, Ingrid and Wendy, inspirators.

The Seal Press
Box 13
Seattle, WA 98111

Library of Congress Cataloging in Publication Data

Wilson, Barbara.
    Walking on the Moon.

    I. Title.
PS3573.I45678W3 1983   813'.54   83-12632
ISBN 0-931188-18-0

Cover design by Laurie Becharas
Book design by Rachel da Silva and Barbara Wilson
Illustrations by Deborah Brown

Table of Contents

9   Il Circo delle Donne

22   Take Louise Nevelson

48   How to Fix a Roof

60   Hearings

72   The Hulk

88   Miss Venezuela

108   Walking on the Moon

for M.

Il Circo delle Donne

The day before I joined the circus I did something perhaps even more out of character. I broke the windshield of two Italian boys who were following me. I was forty-one years old, a housewife and mother of two. I was on my second honeymoon.

The rock hit the windshield with a sound like a flock of birds rising unexpectedly out of the grass, raucous, high-pitched, explosive. Immediately the boys inside began to shout, even before the last cracks had spread, with alarming finality, across the curved front window of their Fiat, and I, a woman who could have been their mother, made a break for it.

I hadn't meant to throw the rock, I'd only meant—but what had I meant? To threaten them? To give them a taste of the same fear they'd aroused in me? Following me like this all over the little holiday town, clutching my arm, gesturing, inviting, suggesting, then getting into their car just when I thought I'd gotten rid of them and creeping after me with their blow-dried, spray-coiffed heads out the window, hooting and whistling. I'd tried ignoring them, had tried explaining, "I'm married," had tried shouting back at them, "Leave me alone"; until finally I'd just stopped, picked up a rock to fit my palm and heaved it in their direction.

The car revved its motor, they were coming after me and now I could no longer pretend I was only strolling vigorously. I started running, tearing down the tree-tented sidewalk as if I were again an eight-year-old girl with a stitch in her side and terror and victory in her heart, two paperboys after her for stealing an evening edition.

I burst into the hotel room. Andrew said, "What's wrong?" I didn't know whether to laugh or cry. My heart pounded harder now I was safe. Surely they wouldn't follow me here, but even if they did—yes, I'd had every right. If I were arrested I'd go with a sneer on my lips, refuse to pay damages. I wished they'd been blinded, maimed for life. . . .

"Nothing," I managed. "I had a slight run-in with some of my admirers."

He raised an eyebrow, yawned and forgot it. Of course no one bothered me when he was around; therefore no one bothered me at all. I was just nervous, I could see him thinking. Judith and her imagination. He tried to rouse himself, lay back down.

"Shouldn't have drunk so much at lunch," he muttered.

We'd had four courses and a full bottle of the local wine, to console ourselves for the weather. It was a gloomy spring here in Italy; in fact, bad weather had pursued us for the last month: unseasonal snow in England, floods in Holland, the mistral in Provence. It was hardly, Andrew had reminded me for the fiftieth time in three weeks, like our first trip to Europe, some twenty years ago—a glowing, brilliant time of picnics in the Mediterranean sun.

I sighed and went to the window to check for the Fiat. I suddenly felt ridiculous, ashamed of my temper. They'd been so young, Greg's age. The street was empty under the new-leafed poplars; behind them was the Lago di Bolsena, a smear of gray liquid that was partly water and partly low-lying fog.

I heard Andrew, also sighing, rise from the squeaky mattress. He went to the sink and splashed water on his face, and

I could see, without bothering to turn, the widely-spaced gray eyes, bland as the lake, the growing bald spot, the too-short socks that showed his thin, hairy ankles, the polo shirt girdling his accountant's paunch.

"I thought we could take a drive this afternoon," he said, gargling Vichy water. "See the cathedral at Orvieto. What do you think?"

"All right."

God, but I was sick of him.

The Umbrian hills were covered with grape vines and orchards just beginning to flower. It was an old, much-cultivated land, I read in the guidebook. The Etruscans were here first, their grave sites still dotted the slopes; they had been conquered by the Romans in 265 B.C. Later the Christians had built their towns on the volcanic mesas, "as close to Heaven as possible."

The town of Orvieto stood up like a hardened sandcastle in the midst of the sunless, blossoming hills. There was a stone bridge leading to it over a trickling river. Just before the bridge, however, was a flat piece of land with a red tent collapsed on it like a parachute and half a dozen painted trailers. I saw an elephant eating poplar leaves, and several black horses.

"Andrew, it's a circus."

"*Il circo delle donne,*" he read slowly from a banner stretched between two trees. "Circus of Women? Now what in hell?"

As we got closer we saw signs of great activity. Someone brought a bucket for the elephant; someone else walked by with a dog on their shoulder.

"Are they really all women?" I asked doubtfully. The figures were dressed in workclothes, not a lowcut leotard or spangled headdress among them.

"In Italy of all places," Andrew said, driving right past it.

I craned my neck back. "You know, I haven't seen a circus for years. . . . Did I ever tell you I used to dream of joining one?''

"You juggle the checkbook pretty well," he laughed.
Need I add, heartily?

"I wish the boys could see this," he was saying half an
hour later in front of the cathedral, as he energetically
snapped the big rose window and the marble columns etched
with tendrils and bas-reliefs.

"They had their chance." For myself I was glad that Andy
considered himself too sophisticated, at nineteen, to be
caught dead with his parents in Europe, and that Greg's lifeguard job made it equally impossible for him to join us. It
wasn't that I disliked my sons, just that I found their teen-age
preoccupations increasingly obnoxious. Their obvious desire
to be free of me hurt, at the same time it reminded me of my
own all-too-brief youthful rebellion.

It was Andrew who missed them. If he wasn't talking
about the weather he was mourning their absence. "The
chance of a lifetime." "They used to be so excited about
going to Europe." They had been, once. So had I. Hadn't we
all gathered around the dining room table night after night
with the maps in front of us, the guidebooks opened up, planning down to the hour which museum we would visit, which
hotel we would breakfast at, which coliseum, church, ruin,
resort, spa, beach, factory, parliament building, castle we
would take in, and in which order? Long before Andrew and
I ever made it, however, the trip had become a joke. Always
there was something to put it off. Not enough money, not
enough experience with languages, Greg's appendicitis,
Andy's drug bust, Andrew's new client. I was the only one
who'd never had anything holding me back.

Which is why I'd been dutifully trudging around for the
last few weeks looking at cathedrals exactly like this one. If I
were by myself I wouldn't be here, I'd be down at the circus
tent, watching them set up. Could it really be an all-women's
circus? I'd wanted to be a lion-tamer, myself, or a horseback
rider. Years and years ago.

My eye wandered across the Piazza to a group of young men in tight rayon shirts unbuttoned to the navels of their hairless chests. Their voices were loud, exhibitive, their gestures full of smoke and contempt. They dominated the old stones of the Piazza; around them, at a careful distance, walked silent women in black dresses, carrying baskets and bundles, their heads down. Andy still expected me to do his laundry when he came home from college. I'd overheard Greg telling a friend on the phone, "My mom says she's for the ERA but she's never done anything with her life."

I started through the wide doorway behind me.

"Wait," said Andrew. Then, "I'll catch up with you."

I hardly heard him, or else I might have asked myself, again, why it was so important that we stick together all the time. Hadn't we spent almost every minute in each other's company for the last few weeks? It was one thing, if you were both twenty-one and just married and desperately in love—as we had been, yes, we had been—to cling to each other like grasshoppers in heat, but after twenty years of marriage and going your own way (Andrew to the office, me to the grocery store, to the PTA, to the swimming pool, to the dry cleaners), what point was there? Especially when you didn't look at anything in the same way and were tired of the very sound of his voice, of his ideas and his fake cheerfulness and his homesickness and his curiosity and his need, and his need.

The cathedral interior was striped in black and white marble, with numerous frescos and carved woodwork. I'd left the guidebook with Andrew; if I'd had it with me I probably wouldn't have opened it anyway. I reserved my cultural interest for my husband's benefit. By myself I lapsed into boredom, a mental lethargy as concrete as the walls of a room in a psych ward, not even padded. I couldn't figure out where I'd gone wrong, or why I'd never done anything in my life except have a family, or why it was only now I felt it.

"Psst," a voice at my side whispered. I glanced over and

saw a young boy with a stylized curl on his forehead and the beginnings of a moustache. *"Americana?"*

"Go to hell," I muttered violently and marched in the opposite direction, to where a group of tourists were standing in front of a painted wall. It was the famous fresco by Signorelli, I recognized, having seen its likeness in the guidebook. A vivid and horrible piece of art, it depicted the end of the world, a place of fire and eclipses, earthquakes and murder. In the sky, angels blew long trumpets to wake the dead, who came walking, skeleton by gaunt skeleton, up from the ground. The colors were burnt orange and sooty black, cadaverous green and bruised white. The expressions in the eyes of the damned were hardly different from those of the saved. They all looked hopeless, driven, and, in some crucial way, condemned and abandoned.

"Signora," began a male voice next to me.

I turned, screamed, "Leave me alone," and saw Andrew at my side, totally bewildered by the failure of his joke.

A few minutes later I was walking down the hill to the circus grounds. "I'm sorry," I'd told him. "I've just got to get away by myself for a minute."

I walked quickly, head down as I'd seen the Italian women do, ignoring all comments. Though I refused to look at the men around me I still felt their presence, a malignant and pulsating cancer of maleness, eating away at me. I was afraid to look up, not for fear of what they might say to me, but of what I might do to them. Smash their windshields, smash their faces, make them leave me alone.

I came to the stone bridge, crossed it, joined a few locals at the rope marking the circus grounds. Closer now, I could see that the workers were indeed women, lifting boxes, leading horses and carrying buckets. There was a light rain falling and it sweetened the strong odor of sawdust and animals and canvas. The women were all shapes and ages, from the little girl in overalls and a gypsy scarf tying up her black curls, to the wrinkled midget with a wise face and humped back, to the six-foot-tall black woman in jeans and a sweater. They seemed to be older rather than younger, though, and this surprised me. I always associated the circus with my own youth, had never thought of it as an occupation, as something that adults did. But here was a woman coming past me, in her sixties by the looks of a gray tail of hair coiled around her crown, and carrying a bucket filled with bloody meat.

She smiled at me and asked a question.

"Non capisco." I held out empty hands.

"English?"

"American."

"Ah. And you come to see the circus. The Women Circus?"

Her voice was low, German-accented. Her eyes caught and held me by their sparkle.

"It's wonderful," I said.

"Come inside," she invited, lifting up the rope so I could pass. She had broad shoulders, muscular arms, she smelled of sweat and blood.

I ducked under but hesitated, "I really can't stay. My husband will be wondering. . . ."

She shifted her bucket, waited, said nothing.

I hovered. "You're going to feed the lions?"

"My friends, my children. I am Marianne, the lion-tamer."

To be able to say that so naturally. "Judith Ellery," I murmured.

"Come with me."

"Oh, I couldn't . . . I have to get back."

She shrugged, winked again and passed on. I was still inside the roped off grounds, couldn't make up my mind to leave. I drew a deep breath, sniffed. Why did it seem so familiar to me? I couldn't have gone to the circus more than once or twice as a child, my mother holding my hand, pointing out the animals, assuring me that the tightrope walkers wouldn't fall, that the lions wouldn't eat their trainers. But when I'd told her I wanted to join, she'd laughed. "Wait and ask your husband," she'd said mysteriously.

Other women passed by me, talking among themselves in different languages. None of them asked me what I was doing. I knew I should leave, but when I looked back at the rope, with all the men hanging over it and making insulting remarks, I couldn't. Maybe everything would have been different if I'd had a girl instead of two boys.

Now the tent was going up. It was crimson canvas, very heavy to be supported on such slender poles. Sagging, wavering, slipping, rising and falling. The women shouted to each other, held firm; a lanky clown rushed up to grab a pole . . . and suddenly I was there too. I smelled sweat and sawdust and animal shit, saw the blackness underneath the tent turn to light. I steadied a pole while the woman next to me pulled hard on a rope. She was Indian, her skin the color of warm sand, her hair black as peppercorns.

I saw Marianne across from me as the tent lifted, her two arms raised as if in praise. She smiled at me, shook her head.

I slipped away.

Andrew and I ate dinner in a tiny trattoria, off an alley that was just a stone staircase. For the first time we seriously discussed going home early.

"Three months is a long time to spend traveling," he suggested. "We could still take the rest of the summer off. Rent a cabin by the lake, do some fishing. Even if Greg and Andy didn't want to be there all the time, they could still come up on weekends."

I pictured myself boning fish, hanging sheets out to air, heating water on the wood stove. "I'm sorry," I said. "I keep feeling like I'm failing you in some way." I meant 'failing myself,' but I didn't know how to tell him this.

We held hands over the cluttered table. "We should have come earlier," Andrew said. "We should have made it a regular thing, every four or five years, to come back. I guess we've forgotten how to travel."

I stared, fascinated, at his gray eyes, remembering how I had loved him, when we got locked out of our hotel in Mar-

seilles and panhandled on the streets all night. We had traded
dreams, had planned the future. Even if we had children,
we'd decided, nothing would stop us from living life to the
full. I didn't know I was already pregnant. I looked at the
bulge under his polo shirt, at his balding head. When had it
happened? He seemed so much older than me. My husband,
the father of my children, I reminded myself. I felt nothing
now, except the desire to get away.

"It's me. You're all right. I'm a wreck. I don't know—
everything gets to me—the weather, the stares, the comments. And yet, I don't even want to go home, it's more than
that. . . ."

"It's the weather," said Andrew, waving at the waiter for
the check. "The weather is spoiling everything."

Yet the sky was clear by the time we came out of the restaurant. Now that we'd half decided to leave this country, it
seemed to be doing its best to please us. The stars were
bright, it was almost warm, the windows glittered with choc-
olates and jewelry. The streets were crowded.

"They look like they're all going somewhere," said
Andrew. Then, inspired, "I bet it's that circus. Want to go?"

"I don't know." I thought of Marianne. There were so
many things I could have asked her.

"Are you tired?" He took my arm.

"I don't know, I want, I want. . . ."

"It's been a long day."

As we drove over the bridge we saw the lanterns strung
through the trees, the big tent glowing like a red lightbulb. I
helped to raise that, I remembered, and was silent.

"Sure?" Andrew asked. "All women. It's hard to believe."

"All right," I said suddenly. "Let's go."

It was as magical as the circus had always been, a fairy-
land of animals and spangles and daring acts. *Il circo delle
donne* had only one ring, but there was activity enough, and
this time I didn't feel that I was missing anything.

First came Katrina, the ringmaster, wearing a tux the

color of a mermaid's glittering green tail. She had short dark
hair and a voice that shook the tent walls and yet was impos-
sibly confiding and friendly at the same time. She spoke in
Italian so I didn't understand her. Fortunately, each act was
also announced with a placard, carried around all sides of the
ring by the midget with the wise and shining face.

Elsa e Grazia! Highwire artists, so alike they must have
been twins, with firm, muscular thighs and arms, not wearing the usual low-cut leotard, but instead, old-fashioned bathing costumes, striped in purple and red. They were so easy
and energetic that I only remembered later that they had
worked without a net, skipping and sliding along the wire as
if it were two feet from the ground instead of thirty.

The Sisters Karenina! Three women with Russian-looking
square faces and thick brows. They brought their black
Arabian horses smartly around the ring, then leapt on their
backs and began a series of stunts, to guttural shouts of
"Hei!" and "Ayah!" They did somersaults on the horses'
wide haunches, flipped from horse to horse, rode them
through flaming rings.

"Not bad," whispered Andrew. My heart was pounding
and my palms were wetting through my dress where I had
them pressed. I was remembering how I had jumped onto
old Betsey's back after returning from the circus that morning and Betsey had herself jumped over her owner's fence, a
real circus horse, and run away down the block.

There were jugglers and acrobats, some fine-featured and
Asian, others Slavic and springy. They threw knives in the air
and made pyramids, spun around the ring like jumping
beans. There was a clown named Alphonsine, loosely knit,
all bones and rolling eyes under her carrot frizz, perpetually
surprised by the failure of her schemes. She had a little dog
who followed her everywhere. "Pipi" she was called, a mon-
grel terrier as big as Alphonsine's black bag, who indeed
seemed to live in the bag and only came out to be liontamed
or to shy away from hoops.

We filed out of the tent during intermission and found a
stand selling sticky candy and espresso. The sky was black

and starry as an old piece of carbon paper held up to a lamp. The lanterns glowed green and red.

"I wish the boys could see this," Andrew murmured. "Did we ever take them to the circus, do you remember?"

I shook my head. I could hardly remember the boys, my sons. They seemed to belong to some strangely vague part of my life. Certainly I had borne them and nursed them and bandaged up their knees. I had listened to their troubles in the same way I'd listened to Andrew's stories of his clients. I had watched them turn into men and have no use for me, nor I for them.

"Did you see the way those Russian women jumped backwards onto the horses behind them, that was incredible!"

Andrew agreed. "The European circus is a very interesting tradition," he said. "Long generations of circus families, intermarriages, usually managed by one person. That's why it's so unusual to see something like this. These women must have broken away from the old family circuses to start this."

"What if they were just ordinary women, I mean, housewives or mothers, who just broke away from their lives and did what they'd always wanted to do?"

"Oh, I doubt that," said Andrew. "Think of the training!" He gave me a quick look and laughed. "Why? You're not thinking of joining, are you?" The idea seemed to amuse him immensely. "How could I explain it to the boys? Sorry, sons, Mama has become a horseback rider in an all-women's circus."

'Wait and ask your husband,' my mother had said.

Sheba! A refined, plump matron with gold teeth, sitting high on Jubub, an elephant the size of a truck. Jubub was graciously lumbering, but not without a sense of humor; when she picked up a little boy in the first row and deposited him in a tub of water, her tiny gray eyes seemed to wink.

And then there was Rebekah, the black woman, now dressed in leopardskins instead of jeans, who cheerfully took on challengers and pinned two men to the ground while twirling another in the air, all without seeming effort.

The mood of the crowd, which up to now had been rowdily good-natured, if contemptuous, changed suddenly. A group of men in the back started shouting and one threw a bottle. It took the arrival of the lions to get everyone back in order.

They came, two lions, three, not in cages but on leashes escorted by Marianne, diminutive and gray-haired. This, to me, was the best part of the evening. She had no whip, she did not seem to force or fear them. "They must be really old," said Andrew, a little nervously, but anyone could see they were not, that it was not age that made them bow to Marianne, but understanding. They did not jump through hoops or climb on barrels. They turned over and over in time to the music, let Marianne lie down beside them, let her put her head next to theirs.

It was chilling, it was magical, it was perfect. I stopped breathing several times, I think everyone did.

Then came the finale, too soon, and Katrina thanked us. Andrew stood up. "Very interesting," he said, but he looked as if he would be glad to get away. The lights went up, the crowd shoved out the doors. I saw the women in their black dresses, heads down, following their men out of the tent; I saw men and boys staring at me. I put my head down too.

That night, in the hotel overlooking the foggy lake, I dreamed that two boys were chasing me. I couldn't remember what I'd done or if I'd done anything. I didn't know if I were a child running from the neighbor boys, a mother running from her sons, or a woman traveler running from her admirers. There was no landscape at first, it was only dark, a dark street lit by lamps high above, that cast small round puddles of yellow in front and in back of me. I was terrified, so terrified that I wanted to wake up. Somewhere in my mind was the remembrance that I had the power to stop this horror merely by opening my eyes, as if it were a fresco of the damned that I could turn away from. And yet I felt that if I did wake up, found I was safe after all, that I wouldn't find what I was looking for. And so I continued to run, in my dream, and gradually the darkness took on shapes. Animals. I was in a kind of jungle and the lamps overhead were really eyes, yellow lion eyes, small benevolent elephant eyes, funny winking dog eyes. Oh, of course, I knew suddenly, I'm at the circus, and as soon as I realized that, I stopped running and stood, in full and brilliant light, surrounded by animals and by the women who trained them. There was a great clapping and, unhesitatingly, I bowed.

I opened my eyes. It was still dark, but I had the premonition of light coming slowly from somewhere outside. I went to the window and watched the sun come up over the lake. It was misty, white, unearthly.

Without making a noise I put on pants and a heavy sweater, took my passport and the keys to the car. At the door I stopped and looked back at Andrew, at a white hairy arm cradling the bald head. A good father, I remembered. The boys will look just like him.

It was about seven-thirty when I reached the red tent. I didn't go up to it yet, but stood by the car in the mist, watching. I saw the woman liontamer, Marianne, she of the gray, coiled hair and muscular arms, who had been on the other side of the tent as it lifted, who had made friends of the lions instead of fearing them, come out sleepily into the morning air with a coffee cup. She yawned, she raised her eyes to the pale sun, she looked around. In the instant before she saw me I thought of my sons, of Andrew, of leaping on Betsey's back. Then Marianne waved and called, "Come," and, unhesitatingly, I went.

Take Louise Nevelson

"You're in Phoenix," Christie said on the phone. "Oh my god."

There was less than delighted amazement in her voice. Melissa paused, unwillingly locking eyes with a teen-age runaway in white shorts and scalloped red boots in the opposite phone booth, before she asked, "Is everything okay? I'm sorry I didn't let you know. I thought I'd surprise you."

"You surprised me all right . . . but never mind, I'll come and get you."

"Are you *sure* this is a good time . . . ?"

"I'll be there in ten minutes."

Half an hour later Christie was at the Greyhound station, explaining nervously, "I couldn't find a parking space."

Melissa, who had spent the intervening time watching the young runaway try to pick up an older cowboy, burst out, "What have you done to yourself? I mean, your hair?"

It was bleached, frizzed and sticking out like a clown's.

"I'm just the same. Oh god, it's embarrassing. When you've known me so long and everything."

"Well, don't worry," said Melissa, hoping for the best. "It looks good."

"It looks like shit, I know. I just got up."

The two friends stared at each other and laughed. Still, it

wasn't quite natural. Just getting up at two in the afternoon? Had Christie been sleeping with someone? Was she living with someone? Her eyes were bloodshot and her tanned face dry and lined.

"I thought this was the middle of the school year?" said Christie. She had always been vivacious, but now her clear, ringing voice had a harder undertone. She rattled her car keys unconsciously.

"I got laid off." For a moment the still-fresh pain of it threatened to overwhelm her, then Melissa said lightly, "Reagan says not to worry if the services in your home town fold up. It's the American way to move on. And the Sun Belt's booming, according to him. So what are you doing these days?"

Christie held open the door of the Greyhound station and the hot desert sun exploded like the flame of a cigarette lighter in their faces.

"Selling encyclopedias," she said.

Theirs was an old friendship, forged in a hated sewing class in junior high. Christie, at that time a skinny misfit with long light brown braids and glasses, had only been slightly better at putting in a zipper than her classmate Melissa, a chubby and withdrawn pre-intellectual. Time had changed them both, but not their friendship. They had gone to college together, on scholarships: Christie to major in art, Melissa to study library science. Ten years ago they'd tried to live together in a cold-water flat in Barcelona, an attempt that ended when Melissa contracted pneumonia and Christie went off with a British lawyer.

In the years since they'd written on and off, seen each other twice—once in London where Christie had set up a studio when Arnold left her, and once in the town near Eugene, Oregon, where Melissa had started a job as a high school librarian. Melissa had tried then to persuade her friend to stay in Oregon.

"It's too rainy, too much like London," Christie had said.

"I want to go someplace really hot, really different."

Phoenix had been her choice, and at first Christie's letters had been enthusiastic. People were interested in her painting, she might get a job in an art school, she had a lover and was thinking of marrying. . . .

"Oh, him?" said Christie tightly when questioned. "The fucker turned out to be already married."

Melissa could have told a similar story, many similar stories of being rejected: Cathy had gone off with Marsha; Pat had returned to New York; and Debra had finally left her the day before she'd been laid off.

She said, "I'm not involved with anyone either."

"Christ," said Christie, pouring her another cup of coffee in her pure white, sparsely furnished living room. "What a pair of losers we are."

Melissa, settling back in an uncomfortable high-tech chair, couldn't help remembering the self-improvement sessions they'd engaged in all through school. Poring over *Seventeen* and later, *Vogue,* they'd endlessly made each other up and curled each other's hair. Melissa had lost weight while Christie had discovered what bold stripes could do for her thin figure and had gotten contacts. Melissa had decided she was the dark, mysterious type; Christie had learned to be bright and chatty.

"I think nineteen was our high point," Christie recalled.

"We were still hanging in there at twenty-three."

At thirty-three both of them seemed to have returned to the body shapes and faces that their genes had marked out for them at birth: Christie was starvation thin, nervous and pinched around the mouth, a chainsmoker; Melissa's heaviness verged on obesity, especially in the hips. If she looked older than Christie it was only because her short dark hair had streaks of white now. But Christie's new style was hardly any improvement. The blonde frizz around her narrow face gave her the brittle falseness of a beauty shop operator.

From coffee they moved on to a bottle of brandy Christie had in the cupboard; from bitter, recent memories they progressed to thoughts of happier times.

"Whatever happened to those watercolors you did on the balcony in Barcelona?" Melissa wanted to know.

They spread the pictures out on the white rug and let the smells and sights of the leafy Ramblas, with its stands of flowers, birds and books, drift into the cool white room.

"We thought we had everything in front of us," sighed Christie.

"Maybe we gave up too easily," Melissa said.

In the morning they both had hangovers that they cured with aspirin and a swim in the apartment pool.

"Hey, this is all right," Melissa said, paddling luxuriously in the clear blue water.

"Phoenix has its good points . . . if you stay off the streets."

"You must be doing pretty well at selling encyclopedias if you can afford this place," Melissa said, noticing the deep lanais around each apartment, the bougainvillea flowering at the edge of the pool, peach, red, violet.

"I'm not too bad," Christie admitted. "My manager says I could bring in three or four hundred a week if I put my mind to it."

"Four hundred a week!" Melissa was astonished.

"But you gotta work your tail off." Christie raised herself out of the pool and stretched out on a towel. Her tan was walnut dark and her blonde curls wept into her eyes. "She had me doing TM, you know, meditation, for a while. To get me centered. I think it helped, but I just couldn't keep it up. I'd be sitting there in the lotus and I'd think, This is ridiculous. So now I go back and forth. I don't go out for a week, sit around and read books and sketch and brood—then I get worried about the rent or the phone bill, and I jump in my car and hustle like a little devil."

"It's hard for me to imagine," Melissa said, swimming over to her side, wondering how long it would take to get a tan like Christie's, how long it would take to lose forty pounds. "I mean, you were always a kind of shy person, underneath." For the moment she forgot Christie's acquired vivacity, remembering only their mutual adolescent pain at being called on in class.

"Oh, it's just like playing a part in a play. This company has the spiel all written out for you. You memorize it and learn to anticipate the responses. Depending on who you contact, you don't have to think about yourself at all. Sometimes I get incredibly high from it, getting people to believe me, getting them to want what I'm selling. And besides," she went on half ironically, as if reciting from a text, "this encyclopedia is a quality product. It took ten years and the work of thousands of experts in their field to develop. It has full color illustrations, up-to-date statistics and detailed maps. It's an invaluable resource for schoolchildren of every age as well as for adults. There are even instructions for all aspects of home repair, cooking and sewing. In only twelve volumes you get a complete library as compared to the hundred or so books you'd need to have the equivalent amount of information in your home."

"Sold," laughed Melissa.

"Maybe I should go out today," Christie said, pinching one of her thin brown thighs in a dissatisfied way.

The first week Melissa stayed with Christie was made up of daily swims, drinks on the lanai and dinners out. It didn't take Melissa long to begin to relax. A vacation was what she'd needed for a long time. She refused to think more definitely about her life. She hadn't given up her house in Eugene or her feelings about Debra; she assumed she'd have to go back and fight the lay-off sometime . . . but right now it was such a relief to be just a guest, to do nothing except wake late, swim, drink beer and eat Mexican food. Even Christie seemed to be relaxing. She still smoked continually and drank a little too much, but some of the old, light-hearted energy had returned. She talked about going back to Europe, about giving art classes. Several days in a row she got out her sketchbook and worked on old drawings.

One morning, however, Melissa woke up and found Christie carefully putting on turquoise eye shadow and skin-tight white pants.

"The day of reckoning is at hand," she said. "Off to the salt mines, or rather, the student apartments down in Tempe. I haven't hit them for a few months."

That day Melissa walked into downtown Phoenix. It was about ninety-five degrees in spite of its being only March, and she seemed to be the only person on the streets. The six-lane boulevards were packed with air-conditioned cars, however; their drivers left them only to dash into equally cool shopping malls or the big, pseudo-adobe buildings in the city center.

Perspiring heavily in her overalls and leather shoes, Melissa experienced dislocation's despair for the first time since her arrival. The feeling here was so different from that of the vaporous green hills and pastures of the Willamette Valley, the muted sky and unobtrusive farmhouses and cabins around Eugene. In Phoenix everything was super-ficial, chain-owned, garish, plastic-shiny—a flat sprawl of gasoline-stinking asphalt on a smoggy dry plain. Melissa had hardly reached the downtown area when she turned back again. She could have cried with longing for the woodsy wet smell of the garden out back, for the small pine bedroom with its view of the hills, for the sound of Debra's voice sing-ing Sweet Honey in the Rock: "B'lieve I'll run on . . . see what the end's gonna be. . . ."

Everything she'd tried to repress about their final argu-ment came back now as Melissa trudged slowly, painfully over the burning bright sidewalks. How Debra had accused her of never wanting to take risks, of constantly lying, of holding them all back by her silence; how Debra had said she would never be a real lesbian until she found the courage to voice it.

"But I don't want to be a *real* lesbian," Melissa had said. "I just want to be me."

It had been the day after Debra left that Melissa had been

called into the high school principal's office to be told of her lay-off. He'd said that the school board had decided that the budget couldn't afford a full-time librarian anymore and that they'd asked a local housewife, a former librarian, to run it instead as a volunteer, with two or three seniors to help check out books. He'd presented it reasonably enough, but there was something in his eyes, and those of the secretaries in the office, that had convinced Melissa there was more to her dismissal than mere budget cuts.

She had offered to reduce her hours, to take a pay cut, had even turned a little sour at the end asking why she was the only one being laid off. Yet she hadn't dared to push it further; she was afraid of being accused, publicly shamed. Had they found out she'd been living with a woman, that she'd had an article published in a lesbian journal, that she sometimes went to gay bars? But I didn't go to the lesbian–gay pride march, even though I wanted to, she thought. I was so afraid of my picture being in the paper. I didn't let myself be interviewed about my work on the library for the women's newspaper. Even though I was the one who started the school's feminist collection.

If she went back to Eugene she'd have support for her fight, but did she really want to fight it, especially if it involved coming out to the school, to the city? What if she lost her house, what if they ignored her in the grocery store, what if she could never get another library job?

"You're kidding yourself if you think everyone doesn't at least suspect," Debra had scoffed. "Why not put an end to their paranoia and save yourself an ulcer?"

"No one suspects," Melissa had said. "No one knows anything about me."

She was the dark, mysterious type.

Melissa was quiet that evening and so was Christie. It had not been a successful day, saleswise.

"Money, money, money," she complained. "They all say they don't have any, but they have Calvin Klein jeans and stereos worth a fortune and their Jags and Saabs are parked all over the street. *We* should have been that kind of poor."

Later Christie had a long conversation on the phone with her supervisor and then announced to Melissa, "I'm going to Flagstaff tomorrow; want to come?"

"What's there?"

"A bunch of untouched students, a Ramada Inn, mountain air. . . ." Christie's voice suddenly took on the cajoling note Melissa remembered well. "Come on, it'll be just like our old times traveling."

"You'll have to promise not to leave me in the lurch then."

"Melissa! Have I ever?"

They left it at that.

The next morning they set off before eight, with styrofoam cups of coffee from Winchell's Donuts, in a brackish fog that lifted only to reveal dismal trailer courts, billboards and desert scrub.

"Take Georgia O'Keeffe," Christie said after a while, lighting a cigarette with a determinedly elegant wave. "Take Louise Nevelson. Now *they* have style."

"You think you'll ever get back to painting seriously?" Melissa asked.

"Oh sure . . . but I was thinking more of their faces, their clothes, everything . . . Nevelson all in black, with those riveting, thick-painted eyes, those turbans. . . . You know, *Seventeen* never prepared us for getting older. We need role models."

"That's true," said Melissa, and felt depressed. Christie, in her tight turquoise jeans, lacy Mexican shirt and high-heeled, appliquéed boots, looked stunningly sexy this morning. But nothing could disguise the bitter lines around her mouth and the dry look of her blonde curls.

"You can say what you want about selling," said Christie, "but in a way it's been good for me. Makes me get out, keep going. I was really dragging around a year ago, let me tell you. Some days I didn't think I was going to make it."

"Because of . . ."

"Randall was the last straw. Up to then I'd still been believing I could make a go of love. Now I just sleep with them and forget it." She stubbed her cigarette out and stared out the window. "But it started with Arnold, that downhill feeling . . . I guess Randall just picked up on it . . . can you believe he told me I was too old for him? He didn't want experience, he wanted a goddamn Brooke Shields."

In London Christie had worn paisley scarves around her head, and gigantic hoop earrings. She had slept on a mattress piled with mirror-studded pillows and soft sheepskins, had burned incense and smoked hash. Her lovers all had two last names and said "bloody bitch" in fake cockney accents.

"Not that I'm interested in love now," said Christie. "Once I get some real money together, I'll go back to painting. This landscape *does* excite me." She gestured to the unprepossessing cacti out the window, then suddenly asked, "So what happened with you? You've never really said. Did you leave or did he?"

"What?" said Melissa and then, uncomfortably, "Oh, I was left. . . ." She paused, wanting to begin, wondering how, murmuring, "It still hurts."

"They're all jerks, men," Christie shrugged. "But what can you do?"

In Eugene Christie had followed her around to women's bookstores and cafes with mixed china and lace tablecloths. She'd talked art with Melissa's current roommate, Pat, and had read some of the feminist books on the shelf. When she'd left she'd admitted that it was all very interesting, but not really her style, and Melissa had realized that Christie hadn't gotten the idea at all.

Now Melissa shook her head, holding back the words as she had held them back so many times before: I'm a lesbian. I love women. I'm a lesbian.

"What are you so afraid of?" Debra had demanded. "No one's asking you to be separatist." But Debra worked in a women's moving and hauling collective; she didn't understand the pressures of being around men and straight women all the time, some of whom would look at her differently, would distrust and disrespect her opinion, would feel *sorry* for her. . . .

"The main thing," Christie said, "isn't really sex at all. It's a matter of style. Take Louise Nevelson, she's like Hecate. Or Isak Dinesen. Have you seen those Cecil Beaton photographs of her? A real aristocrat."

All that Melissa recalled about these women was that they were terribly skinny, gaunt even, but Christie rushed on, "They *made* themselves look like that, totally unordinary, remarkably beautiful and strange, through force of will. That's all, force of will."

By the time they reached the mountains they were back on their favorite adolescent subject: how to change their self-image.

"I just don't feel attractive anymore," Melissa admitted. "Being this heavy. Maybe it influences how I act."

"You were pretty popular in high school after you lost weight."

Melissa hadn't thought about that for years. She would have been ashamed to admit to any of her Eugene friends that looking attractive and being popular was anything to be proud of. In Eugene all her friends were comfortably bulky too. They bragged about their muscles like longshoremen. She'd enjoyed it, believing she had gotten completely away from the rigid stereotypes of what women were supposed to look like. Now she wasn't so sure.

"In London," mused Christie, "I thought I really had it down. Boy, was I hot shit—a cosmopolitan American artist living with an upperclass British lawyer, excuse me, *solicitor.* We used to go to the ballet and the Royal Shakespeare Company, we took our vacations, our *holidays,* in Mallorca. I was such a fool not to marry when he wanted to. I thought I was being so liberated. . . . I never suspected he would change."

Melissa knew that was the price you paid when you identified with a man; she'd read it, heard it and experienced it herself, but her friendship with Christie made it hard to say out loud. Besides, it *was* sad. In spite of being mad at Christie so long ago for ditching her in Barcelona, she'd still been admiring. "My friend who lives in London, the painter, we grew up together. . . ." It was the image still Melissa wanted to have of her—exciting, worldly, artistic.

The mountains were much more beautiful than the desert. Smoky blue even close up, they suggested Indian myths and magical transformations.

I could still change myself, Melissa was thinking. I don't have to be stuck in this body, these attitudes. Lose weight, get a good tan, invest in some clothes, become a traveler again. Of course it would take money and she didn't have much of it . . . but to be free of the expectations, the limitations of Eugene, to find other friends, another life somewhere else. . . .

"What do you think about trying to sell some books with me today?" Christie suddenly suggested. "I could give you some of the easier routes. It'd be a hundred in your pocket, no sweat."

"Oh, I couldn't," said Melissa. "I'm not dressed for it. . . ." She was wearing her overalls, an *off our backs* T-shirt and a pair of worn sandals with socks.

"Nothing easier," Christie laughed. "I've got Mastercharge, Visa, American Express. It would be a pleasure to get you some new clothes. I haven't said anything, but you've let yourself go a little. You could be really attractive with a tiny bit of work."

In spite of herself Melissa was intrigued. Selling, she could never sell, especially encyclopedias . . . but what had she been thinking just now about changing her life? Surely that meant taking some risks. And the money would come in handy, she'd been spending more than she should.

Flagstaff was small and surprisingly rural. The fresh azure sky blew through the car windows with the scent of a dry pine sachet. When they reached the city Christie drove right to the shopping mall.

"Please," she said, when Melissa continued to protest; "my treat. It'll be just like old times."

Growing up in southern California they had spent whole afternoons in the local shopping center, going from one store to the next, trying on wardrobes, discussing them. Green had been Christie's color, emerald green if she could find it; it went best with her long, sunstreaked brown hair. Plum or maroon suited the darker Melissa, they'd decided. It made her look pampered and wealthy. Melissa had worn Maybelline Velvet Brown eyeliner and mascara, Christie Jade Green. They'd had their favorite perfumes as well—Chantilly for Christie, Wood Musk for Melissa—though they'd never been able to afford anything but a spray from the tester bottle.

"This is really ridiculous, you know," said Melissa, but she let Christie lead her inside the most expensive department store, let Christie explain to a haughty-looking saleswoman what they were looking for. It was more than ridiculous, it was embarrassing to admit she now wore a size eighteen. When Melissa put on a dress, her stocky, thickly haired legs looked like a bear's. She tried to explain that even at the library she just wore overblouses and jeans.

"Never mind," consoled Christie. "Have a go at this suit instead."

Finally one of the pantsuits fit and even looked good on her. It was plum-colored and expensive and made her look youthfully mature.

"Don't worry," Christie said. "None of your friends will see you. But you look fantastic."

Christie bought a pair of designer jeans and a shirt for herself, signing the Mastercharge slip with a disdainful flourish. As they came out of the store she linked arms with Melissa, laughing, "Oh, that was so much fun. I've missed having a girlfriend."

"I've missed you too," said Melissa.

They ate lunch at a pleasant restaurant waving with ferns and had several glasses of wine, while Christie explained all Melissa would need to know about the encyclopedias. It was easy to fall in with Christie, especially while drinking, and to believe she could really do it. Once outside the restaurant, however, as Christie was driving her to the area she was to canvas, Melissa experienced strong misgivings.

"How can I knock on anyone's door? I hate people knocking on mine."

"Don't be silly," said Christie impatiently. "Just remember what I told you. They'll eat it up." She gave Melissa a pat before shoving her out the car door. "I'll meet you at that Ramada Inn over there in five hours."

Even before one half hour had gone by Melissa knew that she wouldn't have any sales. It was all she could do to merely tap gently on a door. When it opened she felt blank.

"Hello," she said miserably. "I don't suppose you'd be interested in an encyclopedia? . . . Well, thanks anyway. Sorry to have bothered you."

The housing area was made up of small duplexes and trailers. These were not rich students like those Christie had described in Tempe. Beat-up sedans lined the dusty streets and broken toys and beer cans clogged the gutters. Few of the residents, all renters probably, had made any attempt at landscaping; occasionally there were spindly trees, more often there was nothing but some shabby, butt-strewn grass and a few tall, flowering weeds around the buildings. The interiors, from what Melissa could see during the brief intervals the doors were open to her, were just as pathetic: shaggy, discolored rugs or worn linoleum, cracked vinyl sofas and bedspread-draped armchairs, plain plastic tables, beer bottle collections or dusty knickknacks along the windowsills. Each time a door opened she had a glimpse into her own past, her own family's way of life.

If she hadn't known it before, she knew it now. She had traveled a long way from her childhood, from a world where cheap shabbiness was the norm, where people were at the mercy of those salesmen who chose to badger them.

For fifteen years she'd been able to forget all that. A scholarship had taken her away to college; two summer jobs had paid for her trip to Barcelona; she'd been middle-class ever since—no, more than middle-class, free to choose her own life. In Eugene she'd become beyond class, able to be environmentally aware because she had money, able to eat simple, nutritional food because she had money, able to dress unobtrusively because she had money. . . .

Now, standing in front of a peeling pastel duplex with cut-rate organdy at the windows and a rusty lawn mower half-hidden in the weeds, Melissa remembered everything. Was this the reason she couldn't come out? Because she was afraid of losing everything she'd worked for, had come to take for granted? But I've lost it, she reminded herself, without calling myself anything. And Debra, the prom queen from Minneapolis who'd become a proud truck driver, hadn't understood. "Are you still hoping you'll find the perfect man, the man who'll make the decision for you?"

"Debra," she'd pleaded. "I love you, I want to live with you. And I am a lesbian, I just don't want to be publicly identified as one. I don't want to be interviewed. I'm afraid of being fired if they realize how I've spent the library budget."

But perhaps it was true, perhaps she was still waiting for the right man to come along, as her mother continued to assure her he would, as she had hoped, as Christie had hoped, in the poverty of their tiny bedrooms, poring over *Seventeen*.

"I don't even know any men," she reminded herself aloud, just as one of the duplex doors opened and a woman stepped timidly out onto the broken porch. She was very young, dressed in a faded halter top and a pair of Levi's. Her hair, silky, blonde, was in rollers.

"Are you selling something?" she inquired nervously. "Because my husband doesn't want any."

"Is he here?"

"No, but he doesn't like me, you know, talking to salespeople."

For some reason this rule made Melissa more aggressive than she'd been able to be with any one else.

"I won't take much of your time," she said persuasively.

"I think it's something you'd really be interested in."

"I don't know." The woman touched her hand to her rollers as if checking for dryness. She was incredibly young to be married, seventeen or eighteen at the most. Her cheeks, though pale, still had a baby fat roundness.

"What's your name?" asked Melissa, coming towards her.

"Jill . . . Jill Peters."

"Jill, you don't mind if I come in for a minute, do you? I'm really not going to try and sell you anything you don't want."

"Well, just for a minute. . . ."

Walking into Jill's house was like walking into a version of Melissa's parents' house, or their house of twenty years ago. Even the smell was the same: stale, cigarettey, sad. There were snapshots taped to the wallpaper, a bowl of wax fruit on the table, a few *Sports Illustrated* and *Family Circle* magazines carefully arranged in a basket. The TV, underneath a plastic doily and a jar of dried weeds, was the center of the room; in a cage by the window peeped a lone canary.

"Been married long?" was all Melissa could think to ask.

"Only three months," Jill said, beginning to unwind her long soft hair from the rollers. "Larry's a student. I'm planning to take some classes too," she added. "When he gets finished. I just found out I'm pregnant, though."

She tried to seem happy, but her round face looked wan and almost ill. The blonde curls fell gently to her bare shoulders. "Can I get you some coffee or anything?"

"Coffee, sure. Thank you." Melissa followed Jill out to the tiny kitchen. It was spotlessly neat, again like her mother's. All those macaroni and cheese dinners, eaten by the light of the Mickey Mouse Club and the Evening News. All those peanut butter sandwiches gorged down at the old plastic table with the shiny checked tablecloth. She could almost remember the pattern of the plates, colored flecks in them like candy.

"What are you selling?" Jill asked, setting a kettle on to boil.

"Encyclopedias."

"That must be fun, going around to people's houses."

"It's all right. This is my first day." Melissa stopped herself from explaining anything more. Better get started, better start with the spiel. She suddenly glimpsed her head in a mirror over the sink. Could this heavy-set, mature-looking woman with the gray and white streaks in her hair be herself?

"What's you husband studying?" she asked instead.

"Oh, just general for now. He doesn't really know what he wants to do. I want to be a nurse . . . someday," Jill said, sitting down and twisting a lock of hair in her fingers. She was polite to Melissa as she would be to any middle-aged woman.

"That sounds good," said Melissa.

Conversation had suddenly faltered. Melissa stared at her hands, trying to avoid the mirror over the sink. What had made her ask to come inside? Jill seemed to be wondering the same thing.

"I don't think Larry would be interested in an encyclopedia. I mean, he does all his studying at the college and everything."

What about you? Melissa could have demanded. Christie would have, even though she was no feminist; she would have started right in convincing Jill that she was able to make a decision on her own. But Melissa, for all her politics, couldn't seem to do that. If, by some miracle, she got Jill to agree, she'd have to live with the thought of what Larry would do or say when he came home. He'd be furious with Jill, just as Melissa's father had been when her mother bought that vacuum cleaner on credit or when she'd enrolled in a correspondence course for bookkeeping. He'd always acted as if her mother were too stupid to take any independent action; she'd ended up believing it herself.

Melissa stood up, murmuring, as if she were frightened of something, "Thanks so much. I won't wait for the coffee."

"All right," said Jill helplessly. "Well, good luck. Have a nice day."

She leaned on the door watching Melissa walk to the sidewalk, twisting and retwisting her long blonde hair in her fingers, a slight figure against the shabby duplex.

I can't let this get me down, Melissa told herself, walking furiously across the street. I can't start empathizing with every woman I meet. Why couldn't I have treated her differently? She expected it. I could have been warm, friendly, authoritative, the graying, mature woman in the mirror. Jill was lonely, it would have been a snap to sell her.

Something nagged at Melissa as she stood on the street corner, wondering which house to try next. Henry Mandell. Someone she hadn't thought about for years, and wouldn't have now but for Jill and the absent Larry. It had been the summer before college, when she and Christie had hung around the community pool, flirting with lifeguards. He'd wanted to get engaged. A tall, muscular boy with a silvery fall of hair across his brown forehead, the handsomest boy she'd ever known. What if she had married him? She might have had three children by now, be what Jill would become in another fifteen years—what her mother was now, a tired, frowsy housewife who was afraid to open the door to strangers, afraid to have a thought of her own.

If it hadn't been for Christie, for the feelings she'd had about Christie even then. . . . "Don't throw your life away, Melissa. Think of everything we want to do."

Melissa found herself at a halt in front of a small house at the end of the block. She couldn't recall where she was in relation to the Ramada Inn any longer. She did want to be able to say to Christie that she'd sold at least one encyclopedia set. She went up to the house and knocked.

A young man in jeans and a Budweiser T-shirt answered the door.

"I wonder if I could take a minute of your time to tell you about something that will change your life?" Melissa said eagerly.

Fifteen minutes later she was still there, still talking vigorously and, she thought, on the point of making a sale. Rob and his wife Sarah were definitely interested. They thought it might be an investment for their two pre-school boys. Unfortunately, Melissa found herself talking more and more to Sarah, telling her what she had been too hopeless to tell Jill. "Think of this as something you can use all your life, something that will help keep you in touch with the world."

At that suggestion Rob put his foot down. "I don't think we'd be able to swing it." His eyes were suddenly suspicious and hard.

Sarah, a quick, curly-haired redhead, said, "But Robbie. It sounds so great. Melissa is a librarian, and Grandma and Grandpa might. . . ."

"I said *no*, honey. Thank you very much for your time, Ma'am, but I don't think we're ready to make that kind of outlay."

Melissa forced herself to smile. "Oh, sure, I understand."

Before the door was quite closed, though, she heard him mutter to his wife, "If she's a librarian, what's she doing selling encyclopedias?"

What did I do wrong? But Melissa knew, as she walked with counterfeit briskness away from the house and toward a series of vacant lots that led up into the pine-sprinkled hills. She'd acted as if Sarah were a person too. If she'd continued to direct her spiel towards Rob she might have made it. It hadn't been consciously intentional—she had almost liked him at first. She was just so used to talking only to women. And now she hated him. Fucking pig, controlling asshole. They were all the same: Henry, who'd wanted her to give up college and marry him; Taylor, who'd expected her to follow him all over the country while he looked for work; Glenn, who'd answered her questions about his job with a 'you wouldn't understand.'

Melissa slowed down, puffing a little, and began to search for a spot to sit on the hillside. No, that part of her life was gone forever, and had been for years, ever since she turned up in Eugene, still smarting from Glenn's rejection. And she was glad it was gone. Whatever her problems with women were and had been, they never centered on the male ego, on

the differing balance of worldly power. Painful as her part-
ings had been with women lovers, difficult as some of their
arguments and disagreements, she felt they'd pushed her forward, in some way, toward honesty and a better understanding of what she wanted and needed—and never toward self-
hatred, the continuing legacy of misogyny.

From her sunny, needle-strewn seat on the hill, Melissa
regarded the mobile homes and rag-tag houses and duplexes.
She wondered idly what Robbie would have done if she'd
declared herself a lesbian. Thrown her out on her ass, probably. "It's important to make a point of it to everyone,"
Debra had said. "To let them know we're everywhere, that
they can't keep making their stupid heterosexist assump-
tions. If they know or suspect and you still don't tell them,
you're playing right into their hands, don't you see? Letting
them see you're ashamed and afraid of their opinion."

Once it had been enough just to come out at all—to yourself, to other women. They'd understood why you didn't
want your parents to know, or some of your old friends, or
most of your co-workers and neighbors. They would only be
upset, they wouldn't understand. Melissa leaned back on the
carpet of warm, sweet-smelling needles and looked up at the
mountain blue sky. She closed her eyes and saw it again, that
dream she'd had just before waking the other morning.

There was a dinner party, in a restaurant, a Chinese restaurant with big, round, black-lacquered tables that reflected
the light. Many of the people at the tables she knew; they
were relatives, they were old friends, some from very far
back. Old boyfriends were there, her first grade teacher, her
mother, her father, her two older brothers, Christie of course,
Christie the way she used to be, with long, sun-streaked
brown hair and an eager, determined face.

There had been a lot of toasting and laughing, and finally
Melissa herself had stood up with a glass in one hand, raising
it high, saying, "Yes, it's true, yes, it's true. I am. I'm a lesbian."

Then what a clapping and murmuring and delighted sighing there had been. It was as if she'd said she just won the

Nobel prize. She had looked at them, everyone, recognized them, loved them, and in turn, felt their acceptance float up over her like warm steam from a bath, had seen the love on every face.

Melissa lay drowsing on the hillside for a while longer, drugged by the warmth and pine smell, making her decision. When she finally sat up, it seemed very still and hot in the dry mountain air. She was dazed but certain; she would start with Christie.

It was just sunset as she approached the Ramada Inn. The sky was pale rose and peach, the air mild with a hint of wood burning. Crickets chirped softly and for a moment Melissa felt happy in spite of her tiredness. She and Christie would have a quiet evening, talking things out. Maybe they'd take a drive to watch the stars. A few were already out; soon the southwestern sky would be full of them.

She found her friend in the cocktail lounge, standing at the bar with two men.

"Melissa, over here," Christie called loudly. "Want you to meet two super guys."

She was more than a little drunk and already somehow physically entangled with one of them. George was his name; he was a strapping fellow about forty or so, with the bold offensiveness of the natural salesman. He was wearing a Hawaiian tie and a gaudy turquoise and silver ring. The other man, Bob, was even slimier, dressed in a blue polyester suit and a pink, striped shirt. He was the short, wizened kind of man who always made Melissa feel huge.

"I didn't do too well," Melissa said, trying not to show her dismay. "Only one sale." It had been to two Kuwaiti students who spoke minimal English and offered her mint tea. They had been very polite and surprised by her visit. One of them wrote out a check while the other chattered on about America and Americans. "You are so free here, you girls. In my own country the girls do never go out."

"Well, that's one more than me. Hell, I gave up after the

first ten minutes. I knew I wasn't up to it." Christie's turquoise eye shadow was smeared and her lipstick had run into the fine lines around her mouth.

"You gave up?" said Melissa, thinking, and you let me trudge around all day by myself?

Christie was oblivious. She lit another cigarette though she still had one going in the bar ashtray. "Some days it's just like that."

"Yap," agreed her companion. "Some days the bar is the only place for us."

"What are you drinking?" asked the small, skinny man, with a repulsive nudge of familiarity.

Nothing, Melissa almost said. Screw off. But she settled for a beer. She didn't know what to do. She'd been, without realizing, desperately looking forward to talking with Christie about the people she'd met, about their shared past of poverty. "Was it really so awful?" she wanted to ask. And, "Did you have the same feeling of escape I did?" "How can you bear to be reminded of your childhood all the time?"

Now a part of her already knew the answer. Christie couldn't. That's why she was drinking. She'd probably been drinking since she dropped Melissa off.

Mingled pity and anger surged in Melissa's plum-jacketed chest so that she could hardly hear Christie's next words, cajoling, intimate. "No reason we can't have dinner with these fellows, is there? Not when fate's thrown us together and all."

It was what she'd said when they were in the cafe in Barcelona. "Melissa, come and meet Arnold. He's staying in the same apartment building we are. It's fate!"

"Count me out," said Melissa. "I'm exhausted. Do we have a room yet?"

"Hey, don't be a spoilsport," said George, hanging over Christie's thin shoulder. "Gal here says you're visiting her from Oregon. Remember you're on vacation."

"Please, 'Lissa. Just dinner, and then we'll go to bed."

"Har, har," laughed George. "I guess you didn't mean that like it sounded."

Melissa felt like she was going to be sick. In Barcelona Christie had giggled, ''Arnold asked me if we were lesbians or something. Can you imagine?''

There were all looking at her. ''Well,'' said Melissa, forcing herself. ''Just dinner then.''

In Barcelona, in the beginning, they had been so happy together. Melissa couldn't remember when it began to change. She herself had been easily satisfied, following a routine of study in the morning over *café con leche*, visiting the sights in the afternoon or leisurely reading the *Herald Tribune* at sidewalk cafes, traipsing from bar to bar in the evening. It was her first real taste of freedom. No more classes, no more books, no more teachers' dirty looks. Just the warm September sun lighting up the Plaza de Cataluña, with its flocks of white pigeons and children in short pants and pinafores . . . the delicious taste of puddingthick hot chocolate with little fried donut rings . . . the late nights when, full of Rioja wine and *tapas* of squid and sweetbreads, she and Christie had strolled back to their flat through the feathered trees of the Ramblas, under moonlight shining on ornate baroque scrollwork.

They had held hands sometimes, had sung old folk songs, and Melissa had felt Christie's long soft brown hair on her cheek, the sweet smell of her, California roses and Spanish Maja. She hadn't minded much when Christie first got to know Arnold and his friends. Manuel and Fernando were Spanish; they'd taught her jokes as well as giving her poetry to read. And after all, she and Christie had always had boyfriends, from high school through college. None of them had stood in the way before.

It was just that, for the first time, Melissa was beginning to feel something different about her friend, something new and exciting and terrifying. It might have been because they were in a foreign country together, freed from the restraints of home—the worries about money and getting good grades, the need to fix on a career, the depressing family visits—that it was happening. Or it might have been happening inside Melissa herself. Perhaps she'd always been attracted to Christie. Perhaps their adolescent involvement with each other had been something more than shared narcissism. Melissa didn't know, but something inside her urged her to hope.

When occasionally Christie expressed dissatisfaction: "We're not meeting anybody"; "Do you think we should travel around a little?" Melissa had always agreed. Was it her fault then, that Christie had discovered Arnold? And yet it still might not have come to anything if Melissa hadn't gotten sick.

It had started with a cold caught in an unseasonal rain and it hadn't gone away. Day after day she'd lain in bed, sneezing, then coughing, feverish, and with a growing pain in her side. It was too much to expect that Christie should always stay with her. Christie had brought her medicine and then a doctor who said Melissa had pneumonia and needed to go to the hospital.

Christie had visited her there up until the day of her release. Then the nurse had brought a letter.

"Melissa, don't be mad. I just couldn't hang around here any longer. Arnold has to go back to London and I've decided to go with him. But I expect you to come and visit us before you go home. Hear? This trip was the beginning of my whole life. Thanks for being such a great friend."

Bob, the weasely salesman, was sullen but pushy. Perhaps he was emboldened by the sight of George already fondling Christie's knee under the table. Bob kept offering to buy Melissa another drink, though she still had most of her beer, and trying out possible conversations while wolfing down steak and fries. He knew all about Eugene, he said. "Not too much night life there. What do you do for excitement?"

"I don't do anything for excitement," Melissa told him, moving her salad around in the bowl. She had stopped trying to catch Christie's eye; her friend was too busy describing her

life in London to George. "I was a designer for a very important ad agency. We had the Mary Quant account and lots of
others. I'm really an artist. David Hockney called me one of
the best American painters to come out of the seventies. I just
thought selling would be fun for a while."

Take Louise Nevelson, Christie had said. Take Georgia
O'Keeffe. Still prolonging the lie that she could become anything but what she was, a cheap, flashy, alcoholic, second-
rate. . . . No, Melissa couldn't judge her. Too many memories
still tugged her back: Christie at thirteen, practicing ballet in
her mother's living room, absurdly dressed in tennis shoes
and a baggy old swimsuit; Christie at fifteen, winning an art
prize for her self-portrait; she and Christie swearing eternal
friendship at sixteen, on the way home from school one day;
testing each other on French verbs, sharing countless pizzas
and confidences, discussing methods of birth control or how
to scrape up money for a job-hunting dress, planning their
trip to Spain.

She was my best friend, thought Melissa, staring at the
thin stranger with the frizzy hair and loud, hectic laugh
across the table. I'll never have another. Not Debra, not anyone. But why didn't she share my feelings? Why did she
leave me for Arnold just when I was learning how to love
her?

"I hate to say this," said Bob to Christie. "But your friend
here isn't giving me a whole lot of help."

Christie and George looked over and Melissa saw George
give Bob a beefy wink. Christie smiled at Melissa impatiently.

"Oh, 'Lissa's a serious girl. Librarian. Dark, mysterious
type, you know. Opposite from me."

"Maybe she doesn't like you," said George to Bob.
"Maybe you're not her type."

"Yes I am," asserted Bob, half angrily. "Any woman's my
type." To prove it he put his hand on Melissa's thigh.

"You get your fucking hand off me," Melissa said evenly.
She stood up and moved out of the booth.

All their faces looked up at her, surprised and unsympa-
thetic.

"Whassa matter?" Bob finally said. "You don like men?"

"No," said Melissa slowly, holding on to the edge of the round black table. "I don't. I like women. I'm a lesbian."

She stared straight at Christie as she spoke and for a moment Christie, robbed of her drunkenness, met her eyes. She knows, thought Melissa; she's always known. It was as clearly as they had ever looked at each other, and as finally.

"Good-night," said Melissa. As she stumbled through the dining room she heard Christie's slurred but ringing voice, "Don't ask *me*. I hardly know her, haven't seen her for *years*."

In the emptily comfortable, regulation-appointed room of the Ramada Inn, Melissa sat for a while on one of the single beds, staring at the phone and at herself in the huge wall mirror. The graying, mature woman looked shaken, but somehow more familiar, even resolute.

"We can be anything we want," she and Christie had always told each other. "We can do anything we want to." It was the chant that had carried them through their adolescence into college and into the world. The litany that had saved them from the lives of their working-class parents. The lie that had left them unable to recognize the strengths and weaknesses they already had, believing that identity was a mask to be put on and taken off at will, nothing to do with who you really were, with what you really wanted from life.

Debra answered at the first ring. "Melissa, I've been trying for days to get you. I've been so worried."

"It's good to hear your voice."

"But where are you? This sounds long-distance. Oh, I've been kicking myself ever since I left. I really didn't mean everything I said. And then I heard you lost your job. . . ."

"No, you were right. It's time for me to choose. I've chosen."

There was a pause; Melissa could hear Debra stop breathing and realized she didn't know what Melissa was going to say.

"I came out," Melissa told her, and the words didn't scare her. "Girl, did I come out."

"But where are you?" Debra's breath came back in a rush of warmth. "When are you coming back?"

"I'm in a Ramada Inn in Flagstaff, Arizona, looking at myself in a mirror. Yeah. But I am coming back. Tomorrow. I'm going to fight the lay-off and whether or not I win, I'm going to leave Eugene for a while." She found herself smiling at the woman in the plum pantsuit. "I'm going to Spain, to Barcelona. I just realized I never finished my trip. . . . Want to come?" she asked.

HOW TO FIX A ROOF

When my cousins and I were little, Aunt Jane and Ma used to joke that we kids had been exchanged in the cradle. They said I should have belonged to Aunt Jane, and Carrie and Darryl to Ma. I always reminded them that I was younger than my cousins, so how could there have been a mix-up?

When I got older I started to understand.

Not that I don't like my mother. I love her better than almost anyone, but she's different from me, or I guess I'm different from her, since she was here first. I mean, look at her: she's tiny and jumpy and always has a quick put-down and an opinion or two or three or a hundred on everything. She wears glasses and has wiry brown and gray hair that she sticks behind her ears when she's thinking. She's organized and political and involved in every cause that comes along, and as far back as I can remember, she's always been like that. Dad's sort of the same way, though he's quieter, and they get along in what Aunt Jane calls a "neurotically whole-some" way.

Aunt Jane's divorced, like I'd probably be if I was forty-eight and not fourteen. We're tall and red-haired and stub-born and we can't get along with anybody, even though underneath we're pretty nice people. Ma calls us "moody."

That's her way of getting back for being called "practical." I used to ask her what she meant by "moody." She always said, "Your Aunt Jane."

Aunt Jane is an artist, though, like I want to be, and I think it's good for artists to be moody. I mean, they have to sit and plan out what they're going to do, and they can't always be worrying about how many people they invited for dinner and what to feed them, or who to call if the toilet gets stopped up, or what new awful thing the government is plotting. It gets in the way of their concentration.

That's what Aunt Jane says when Ma tries to talk her into something, like going door to door to stop the arms build-up, or making cookies for a bake sale to benefit somebody. "I have more important ways to spend my time, Madeleine," she says. "And don't bother making me feel guilty either."

Cause Ma is good at that. "More important things than peace?" she shrieks.

I tried to tell Ma once that carrying picket signs interfered with my concentration too, but she told me I was too young to have any concentration and what kind of world did I want to grow up in anyway?

When I go over to Aunt Jane's house she leaves me alone. I go right to my part of her studio and start laying out my paints. Her studio is in the attic, the whole length and width of the old house that Ma and she grew up in and that Aunt Jane has lived in on and off during her whole life. It's so quiet up there and you can see across the lake to a little island where Aunt Jane and Ma used to picnic as kids, and the sunlight comes in, through the big glass windows that frame one whole wall. We can work there for hours and then, when it gets dark, we'll take our pictures downstairs and prop them up against the sofa (which is spotted with paint already so it doesn't matter) and discuss them.

Aunt Jane cares what I think, she says I have a good eye for color, unlike Ma who asks me, "Is this punk or what, these plastic pink shoes and where'd you get that purple sweater, good god, with your red hair!" After we're done looking at the paintings, Aunt Jane has a glass of Scotch and I have some milk and sometimes we eat smoked oysters and cheese and crackers, which is all Aunt Jane has around.

Sometimes Aunt Jane tells me stories and they're always different from the ones Ma tells me. Ma's version of her early life is that she was a good student and wanted to become a nuclear physicist but then she met Arnie (my dad) and he was a radical and a pacifist so she realized she should do something else. Like cause trouble. To hear her talk you'd think she never was a kid at all or had any fun because she was too worried.

But Aunt Jane has other memories. Like how Ma got sent home from school for putting tar on the teacher's seat and how she used to hang out in the bathroom rolling her hair for hours. And also how the two of them were always together in the summer, swimming and rowing to the island for picnics and trying to catch fish with safety pins.

Ma has never denied any of this, but she sighs when I bring the stories up and says, "Oh that was so long ago." And she says that Aunt Jane should never have moved back to that house after Grandma died because there are too many memories . . . and besides, it has a leaking roof, it always did, and someday Jane'll fall down those attic stairs and break her neck like Grandma (Grandma just broke her hip, but then she got pneumonia in the hospital, so Ma considers it the same thing).

What I like best though is when Aunt Jane tells me stories of her life before she came back here, when she lived in Paris and Tokyo and Los Angeles, "when it was still a nice city, hardly smoggy at all."

"I wish I was an artist in Paris," I said.

"But I was never an artist there, just a bum, we were both bums, it was lovely." Later on Harry, my ex-uncle, got a job in Tokyo with the government. "Never marry a bureaucrat," Aunt Jane warned me, "even when they appear to be a bum at first."

"I'm never getting married," I said.

"Good girl."

Ma always says, "Oh, you'll grow out of *that*."

In Los Angeles Aunt Jane started to paint and got a little famous, she says because of her red hair and her mean personality, but also I think because of her work. Even Ma is proud of her, in her way, especially since Aunt Jane moved back to our city. "Jane Delorio?" I'd heard her tell someone. "She's my sister."

She's my *aunt,* I thought, and then felt ashamed. It was like I was happier to be connected to Aunt Jane than my own mother.

Because I don't want to make Ma jealous, a lot of times after I come home from Aunt Jane's I make a special effort to help her address envelopes and make phone calls. But my heart just isn't in it. I'm too excited thinking about the painting I finished and what Aunt Jane said and all the things I want to do in life and all the places I want to go.

Sometimes Ma looks sad and says, "I suppose you won't be hanging around here much longer, will you? You'll be off to New York or someplace in a couple of years."

When Aunt Jane suggests that I study in New York I get thrilled, but when Ma says it, I feel guilty. "I could go to art school here," I tell her.

"I don't want to hold you back," she says, but I know she's thinking of Carrie and Darryl, my cousins, and how they're such loyal and unimaginative kids, even if they're not half political enough, that they'd never think of leaving town except for a vacation to Hawaii.

Carrie is getting a graduate degree in the School of Engineering and Darryl has a job in a bike co-op. We used to row out to the island when we were little, but now I hardly see them except on holidays. Ma says they are very bright, but I think they're boring. Aunt Jane sometimes gets mixed up and calls them "Carryl" and "Darrie."

I had just started the ninth grade when things changed. Even though it's only been a few days now, everything seems different. Maybe if I write all the changes down first it won't be so hard later on to explain them. Ma calls this prioritizing but I don't know what's most important so I'll just make a list.

1. Ma went to jail.
2. Aunt Jane fell down the attic stairs and broke her ankle.
3. A big storm blew away some of Aunt Jane's roof.
4. I learned something useful.

You see what I mean about prioritizing? This is sort of the order everything happened in, but some things happened independently and some things happened because of other things.

Everything was important.

But to start out, I'd have to say that having Ma in jail was the most exciting thing. It's because of something she did last summer, when she and a bunch of her friends were arrested for "resisting arrest." At the time I wondered how, if she were really resisting, she could get arrested, but I guess the judge didn't see it that way.

"The Constitution allows for peaceful assembly," he said at the trial. "There were hundreds of people at this demonstration, most of whom dispersed without incident. Only five of you decided you had to make an issue of it by striking members of the police force."

"I'm never going limp again," shouted Ma unexpectedly. "I wish I'd given him two black eyes. Calling me an old lady who should be home knitting!"

So on top of two weeks for resisting arrest she got another one for contempt. The judge said she should be ashamed of herself.

Aunt Jane sat beside me at the trial, groaning loudly and muttering, "Madeleine you fool," but when I asked her whether she thought Ma was a disgrace to the family, like the judge said, Aunt Jane said, "Certainly not. I'm very proud of her. He's the one who's a disgrace."

She told me I should stay with my dad in his hour of need, but as soon as she got home she fell down the attic stairs and broke her ankle and I had to go over there anyway, which is what I really wanted to do.

I don't think Dad has ever known an hour of need in his

life. He's too busy going to meetings and there are even more of them since Ma went to jail. He's pretty happy about the whole thing, he says it reminds him of the Sixties.

But anyway, Aunt Jane was in a terrible lot of pain from her ankle and the doctor said she had to stay off it for at least two weeks. Fortunately both Carrie and Darryl happened to be in Hawaii so it was up to me to take care of her. I brought over all my stuff and started baking cookies right away. I have made thousands of cookies in my short life, mostly for Ma's benefits, and consider it one of my great accomplishments, next to basketball and painting.

I thought it was going to be wonderful staying with Aunt Jane and having her all to myself for two weeks, and after she ate some of my chocolate chip cookies she thought so too. We planned how we would turn the living room into a studio and rig up her easel so she could paint sitting down. It was too late to do anything about it that first night though, especially since we'd eaten so many cookies, so we decided to wait until the next day.

Just as I was lying down to go to sleep upstairs I started to hear the wind getting really loud. The big trees near the house were howling like wolves with sore, cracking throats. The windows rattled and clattered and an unfastened one in the bathroom kept banging open and shut. Then the rain came down, sheets of it like thick, hard plastic with a knife edge, cutting slashes in the night. Slash, crash, bang, rattle, boom. I liked hearing all the noises, curled up under Grandma's quilt, snug and warm. I even heard the lake a few blocks away, slapping like thunder on the shore.

When I woke up the next morning it was still raining, not so hard, more like the usual Northwest blecko. I could have almost forgotten about the storm except that when I came running out to the bathroom (being as usual late for school), I saw a stream of water gurgling down the attic steps. For a minute I just watched it, fascinated by the artistic way it pooled itself up on each step before making the next descent, like a waterfall in a Japanese garden—then it occurred to me that so much water wouldn't just come from anywhere except an overflowing bathtub or the sky, and there wasn't a bathtub in the attic. There was only Aunt Jane's studio.

Or what had been Aunt Jane's studio. I couldn't believe that I'd slept through what must have happened up there during the night. There were overturned chairs and boxes; the easel was lying on its side like a fallen scarecrow; there was a pool of rainbow-colored water an inch deep in the middle, with sketch-boats sailing back and forth in the wind. There was a gap the size of the couch in the roof and it was letting in the rainy sky like there was a shower nozzle up there.

I didn't even stop to think. I rushed crazily down the wet stairs screaming, "Aunt Jane, everything's ruined. The roof is gone, the roof is gone. Your paintings are *ruined.*"

"If I hadn't been taking codeine," said Aunt Jane later that day, "you would have given me a heart attack."

I couldn't understand what was wrong with her, why she just opened her eyes and looked at me like I was somebody in a dream.

"I thought you were a dream," she said. "I wish you had been."

Finding I couldn't wake her I raced back upstairs to try to save whatever I could. It seemed hopeless at first. Even the paintings hanging on the walls were damp; even the sketches lying on the still upright table were soggy and mushed together. Still, I did what I could; I started staggering down the slippery steps, the heavy canvases in my arms. It was only when I dropped one that Aunt Jane woke up.

"Rosa!" I heard her call. "What's going on up there?"

This time I was more careful. "Uh, nothing, Aunt Jane. Just a little . . . rain."

In trying to pick up the canvas I somehow pushed it over the bannisters of the main staircase. It settled with a final crash at the bottom of the stairs, right where Aunt Jane could see it.

"Flaming Venus!" she gasped. I thought she was cursing maybe, but it turned out to be the name of the poor painting, a prizewinner she was getting ready to ship to a museum in

Dallas. Soggy Venus would have been better now.

"Aunt Jane," I said, appearing suddenly to prevent her making any fast moves of rescue or anger. "Your roof's leaking."

"It's always leaking," she said, attempting to stand and falling back with a cry of pain. "But why are you throwing my painting around?"

"I mean, it's really leaking this time. I mean, it's sort of gone."

That whole morning is a bad memory. I ran back and forth, trying to save as many paintings as possible, while Aunt Jane rolled around like a wounded cow on the sofa and shouted directions. "Don't drop anything!" And then she would cry, "Oh, why did I break my ankle? Oh, why didn't I get that roof fixed? Oh, why why why do these things happen to me?"

I wished so much I had Ma to call up. She would have been mad and blamed it all on Aunt Jane, but she also would have known what to do. I kept trying to think of what that would be.

"Maybe you should call somebody, some roof-fixer," I said, on one of my trips down.

"I don't know any."

"Look in the Yellow Pages!"

But the next time I came into the living room with a wad of sketches and a five-by-six canvas, she was still sitting there, carefully sponging droplets of water off the heavy dried oil surface of "Window on the Skagit."

I was glad she'd stopped groaning but I still wanted some help. Plus she'd never asked me about my paintings (they were mostly okay). I hardened my heart. "Well, what'd they say?"

"I can't call," she said abstractedly. "I can't concentrate."

"Oh here," I said, grabbing the phonebook from her side. "I'll call."

"I can't stand talking to those kind of people anyway,"

she muttered. "I've never been able to deal with them. That's why I have an agent. Oh god, what's *she* going to say?"

"Résumés, retirement, rockeries, roofs, roofings. There are millions of them."

I started dialing at random.

"Hello," I said. "We need a roof, I mean, the old one blew away and it's a terrible mess."

"Tell them I don't have much money," Aunt Jane commanded.

"We want it done cheap and as soon as possible."

Aunt Jane yelled in my ear, "Right away."

"Friday?" I said. "Can't you come today? No, I'll try calling some other places."

"This would have to happen when your mother's in jail," said Aunt Jane.

"Well, it did," I said. "So it's up to us."

But really it was up to me since Aunt Jane was back to dabbing at and murmuring over her paintings. Finally I got a roofing person to agree to come over in the early afternoon.

"By that time we could fix it ourselves," said Aunt Jane, who still thought she had a right to an opinion. "Are you sure it's as bad as you say, Rosa? I have some big plastic bags in the basement . . . maybe you could just get on a ladder and stick them in the cracks. . . ."

"You must be crazy," I said, hearing Ma's voice come out of my mouth.

The roofers showed up about two in the afternoon. By that time I'd moved most everything in the studio down to the living room. It turned out that only one painting (that Aunt Jane had never really liked) was badly damaged, but Aunt Jane, instead of being glad, just got more and more distracted. "The work of months," she kept saying. "The work of years."

She was completely into it, and I couldn't help remembering how Ma always said she was too dramatic.

"I don't go around punching cops, Madeleine."

It wasn't that I didn't like either of them being dramatic, but for the first time I started wishing for a little sense and know-how. I was an artist too. How come I got stuck with the details?

The roofers were two guys in overalls and punk band T-shirts. One of them I knew from a long time ago. He'd been a friend of Darryl's in high school and had gone swimming with us in the summers. Aunt Jane didn't remember him at all, but he remembered both of us. His name was Shawn, and his partner's name was Bill.

"I'm glad you finally got here," said Aunt Jane bad-humoredly. "Thousands of dollars worth of art has been ruined."

"It got ruined in the night," I added, so they wouldn't feel it was their fault.

"We'll see what we can do," said Shawn cheerfully.

"I'm not spending a lot of money on this," warned Aunt Jane.

"We can give you an estimate," Bill said. "These are sure beautiful paintings."

But that just got Aunt Jane started again. "Why me?"

I went upstairs with them, trying to excuse my aunt. "It's only that she broke her ankle yesterday, and my mom went to jail and everything. . . ."

"I saw that in the papers," said Shawn. "An inspiration."

I beamed. "Yeah, she's alright."

They both whistled when they saw the roof. The hole seemed to have gotten wider since I'd last been up there; it was the size of a Volkswagen now. Luckily the rain had almost stopped, but the pool in the middle of the room hadn't gotten any smaller.

"These old houses," sighed Bill. "Nobody ever keeps them up."

"I remember playing up here," said Shawn. "How old are you now, Rosa? Seventeen, eighteen?"

"Fourteen," I said.

He looked disappointed. "Well, Bill, what do you think?"

Bill shook his head. "We can throw a patch on her, but it won't hold long. The whole roof looks rotten to me."

"Don't call it her," I said.

"That's right," said Shawn hastily. I thought he had improved a lot in seven or eight years. He used to be one of those skinny boys with glasses. Now he had a gold ring in one ear. He didn't look like a bureaucrat, or a bum either.

"Alright, Rosa," grinned Bill. "We'll need our ladder and something to get rid of this water first. You want to help?"

"Six dollars an hour," I said. I might be an artist, but I knew my value. Even if I'd never fixed a roof before.

We worked the whole afternoon, draining the water from the floor and putting up plastic over the hole. I showed them right away that I was just about as strong as they were and that I had some good ideas too. I learned a whole lot and liked it too. The only bad part was realizing that Aunt Jane was going to cause a stink over how much money it would cost to fix the roof.

"She's not very practical," I told them. It was an understatement.

"Two or three thousand dollars! But I'm only an artist. That's as much as I make in a year sometimes."

"But you must have insurance," Bill said.

We were all back in the living room, surrounding the sofa where Aunt Jane lay like a martyr with her foot in a cast and a moody look on her face. "Oh shit," she said. "I was planning some kind of trip in the spring. Why do these things have to happen to me?"

Once I'd thought it romantic that Aunt Jane had had so many things happen to her. I'd always compared her, favorably, to Ma, who was more likely to make things happen. For the first time I started to wonder what was wrong with Aunt Jane anyway.

We all just sat there and then Bill and Shawn got up to leave.

"Well," said Aunt Jane. "What can I do? I'm crippled, my work of half a lifetime has vanished—I might as well destroy myself financially too."

"We'll start in the morning," said Bill, and Shawn smiled at me. "And if Rosa wants to keep helping. . . ."

"Rosa's an artist," said Aunt Jane. "She doesn't know anything about roofs. She's like me."

"I could learn though," I said, wondering if Shawn would give me a ride to jail to visit Ma. She'd probably like him, if she didn't think he was too punk.

Already I saw myself a famous artist. With a roofing business on the side.

Hearings

The threshers came in from the fields and he a small boy then, not more than six or seven . . . but how well he remembered it . . . the rough trestle tables laid end to end under the oak trees . . . for naturally the kitchen couldn't hold them all, and the heat . . . three women, his mother, no, his aunt and two neighbor ladies cooking all day on a wood stove, pies and biscuits, fricaseed chicken, basins of mashed potatoes with gravy, pitchers of milk so cold it stung your hand to hold them, frothy beer and even coffee in all that heat . . . four times a day they ate, early breakfast at four, late breakfast, then dinner and supper . . . and they were big men, these farmers, with arms like knotted tree boughs, coming in from the fields of wheat, up to the pump to splash their sunburned faces. . . .

I never thought I wouldn't be a farmer. . . .

His daughter murmured something and he turned his head irritably.

It's not my fault, she thought. How am I supposed to remember if it's his right or left ear? Christ!

"This looks like the place, Dad," she repeated.

"Hmmm."

What a stupid idea this all was. But what else was there to do on a visit but be a tourist? And she had suggested it. "Remember that place you and Mom took us . . . once, I can barely remember it. Trees and plants and oh, a wonderful tram with red-and-white-striped awnings. Kevin and I thought it was fantastic."

"The Los Angeles Arboretum," he'd said promptly, surprising her. Had she thought it was a dream?

He was not such a cold man, after all, she decided. She would stop short at calling him tender. What was it he'd put in his last letter? A list of people who'd influenced him: a teacher, her mother, a friend, his second wife. Then he'd mentioned his cat, the cat she'd fucking given him one year long ago when she left the city. And at the end, a P.S.: "I haven't listed either you or Kevin because I feel you've had no influence on my life."

All these years she hadn't seen him and still it hurt. She'd joked about it with her friends. "His cat, for Christssake."

And not me.

She pulled into the parking lot. "Okay, we're here."

That was the trouble with Kate. Always so abrupt. "Okay"; "All right"; "So what?" "Come on." He didn't know where she'd gotten it from. This new job she had, what did she call it—coordinator?

"So you're the boss?" he'd asked.

"No, I'm not the boss. We don't have bosses. It's a collective and coordinator is a revolving position."

Exasperation mixed with triumph, that was Kate all over. And how could he keep up with any of it? When they invented a word a week. But they were too self-conscious to be directors, governors, presidents any more.

All the same he remembered her as a little girl, his peanut Kate. "My Daddy's the President of the California 'Counting Soci-ety." At conventions she had jumped in everyone's lap, had stood on the table and sung a little song.

He didn't dare remind her of that.

She watched him get slowly and painfully out of the car, straighten up inch by inch.

Oh god, he's old.

She remembered his voice on the phone. "I guess I've had a stroke."

He had sounded exactly the same, only a little weaker. He wasn't paralyzed, was he?

No. It was just the hearing in his left ear. Some blood vessel had burst, blocking the tympan membrane. He'd lost his equilibrium briefly. It had come back. So would the hearing, he hoped.

She had never known her father to complain; he wasn't that sort. Whatever happened, he went on.

Still, this was serious.

"Do you want me to come down?"

"No, no. It's really not necessary. I'm fine."

"I want to. Please."

The dictionary said the tympan membrane "closed externally the cavity of the middle ear and functioned in the mechanical reception of sound waves and in their transmission to the site of sensory reception." It was the eardrum; the thin sheath that kept the outer and inner separate, in balance.

Preparing to leave she had talked about it to her friends. "My father had a stroke!"

It was her first intimation of old age. It wasn't fair that it had come to her so early. She hadn't accomplished anything yet . . . she didn't have anything she could call her own. She'd be an orphan if he died . . . an orphan at twenty-nine, no, she supposed not. But she was frightened.

He couldn't die before she'd seen him, told him . . . what?

He was wearing a natty blue polyester suit with a red string tie. His face was firm, though pale, and his hair was entirely white.

"This doesn't look familiar at all," he noted, looking around.

He followed her through the turnstile, watched her scrabble in her pocket for the admission fee she insisted on paying herself. Always so proud; almost thirty and no career. But she had been like that, doing what she wanted, he'd had nothing to say about it.

He felt timid around her.

She wasn't like her mother at all. And in an instant . . . yes, the arboretum, once they got inside, was just the same . . . he saw Polly, dimpled and shy, in a blue serge suit with padded shoulders, exactly the way she'd looked when he first met her at the dance. He'd cut in, could still remember the big, warm sound of the Jimmy Dorsey tune, "You're a Lucky Guy" . . . it was just after the war, in one of those salty old halls down by the amusement park, torn down now, urban renewal and a string of condominiums. She'd been a schoolteacher. A good family and he couldn't say that hadn't helped him get where he was going . . . "You're a Lucky Guy," she'd sung along with the music . . . and the war was over . . . they'd both come out to California to make a new start. "My diamond in the rough," Polly used to call him. But he'd made a good home for her and the children . . . more than he'd ever hoped to do for himself back on the farm when his mother first and then his father had died, forcing him to find a job to get through school . . . but he had done it, and when he heard he got a scholarship he had walked across Illinois to the college because he hadn't had enough money for trainfare . . . "You're a Lucky Guy" . . . they did the foxtrot then and he had stumbled . . . Polly had changed his luck . . . she had expected him to lead and he had . . . he had . . . but where was Kate taking him? She was walking too fast.

She wanted to find the tram. Oh, she remembered it clearly, with its open sides that let you just sail along, looking at everything. She couldn't have been more than eight, at the most, and probably younger, because after her mother got sick they'd never gone anywhere anymore. Not as a family, at least; it had been neighbors and friends taking them along, in cars filled with dozens of kids, no special privileges, the pocket money doled out firmly and "Make sure you go to the bathroom first." Kevin had been lucky, Jimmy next door was just his age, but she had been lonely, taking a book with her everywhere and feeling too good for the rest of them.

Even then.

Pity for her child self struck her. She'd been so glad to finally become an adult . . . but what had she done with it? Time had seemed to stretch out before her . . . she remembered being twenty forever, longing to be twenty-one . . . and twenty-five had felt like a watershed, the moment when she would finally. . . .

"Don't walk so fast," her father told her grumpily. "Didn't you say there was a tram here? I don't remember it. . . ."

You could have been a grandfather, she almost told him, and suddenly she could have cried, though she hadn't cried at all at the women's health clinic. There'd been some blue-grass music on the radio and posters on the walls celebrating and defending women's right to choose. Would she have chosen differently if she'd known her father was going to have a stroke? But who could know . . . who could have predicted that the thought of him dying could have affected her like this . . . make her feel about ten years older overnight and full of the saddest kind of anxiety about his life, her life, the things they had never done or said. And she was forgetting anyway, he already was a grandfather. . . . Kevin's two, the third one coming in a few months. Where *was* Kevin, if it came to that? She could have used his support at a time like this. He was their father, their only father. . . .

"Oh!" she said involuntarily. It was the tram. "But it's so small and faded."

It was all coming back to him. They had gotten off the tram and walked over a bridge. A kind of lake, with ducks, and at its edge, an old Victorian-style house.

"No, there can't be a house here, Dad," Kate told him. "This is all part of an old rancho or something. There might

be some adobe houses, somewhere. Yeah, I think there were
. . . Kevin and I played Indians. . . ."

But he was sure of it. Because he remembered that at the
time it had reminded both him and Polly of her parents'
home by the lake in Michigan, all gables and curlicues, the
house where they had gotten married. She'd come down the
stairs, she'd been carrying Lilies of the Valley and in her dark
hair she had worn a wreath, a wreath . . . and without wanting to, he saw her in the coffin, surrounded again by flowers.
No, I don't want to die . . . that had been his first thought
when he came to at his desk, blood drumming in his ears and
a weightless, numb sensation in all his limbs. He'd tried to
stand, had fallen onto the carpet . . . this is death, was all he
could think, and it couldn't help surprising him, that it was
both so easy and so final, that it had come so quickly. The
doctor said now he could live another twenty years if he
were careful . . . it had been a blood disorder as it turned out,
too many red blood cells, he had forgotten the medical name,
but the cells had built up and built up until they clogged. The
doctor, a woman with a sense of humor he did not appreciate, compared his veins to a faulty sewer system . . . and
now she was saying that he might never get his hearing back
. . . but she had said he might always have to walk with a
cane and look at him now . . . of course he did get tired easily. . . .

And Kate was urging him off the tram. "Let's go see the
herb garden."

She thought it might cheer him up. Honestly, he was
starting to look a little down in the mouth . . . she supposed
they'd have to go soon, and really, what did it matter? They
weren't going to be able to talk, they never had . . . she didn't
feel like shouting into his good ear, "What was your life
really like? How did I fit in? What made you give up on me
and Kevin? It's true you never tried to tell us what to do, but
maybe we could have used some advice. . . ."

The herbs were sweet and pungent. She couldn't help

pressing her nose into a bunch of warm sage, breathing in the dry mountain smell. And for a moment she could have cared less if they talked. Maybe it was just enough to be together, like this, walking in the sunlight, noticing the world . . . why should she always feel a sense of failure with her father? He seemed to expect nothing of her . . . she knew he loved her . . . it was just that she didn't impinge upon his own life anymore, if she ever had. . . .

That time when Robin had accused her of harboring a death obsession and she had denied it . . . but she had been trying to finish her first novel and had developed a strange fear of crossing the street . . . she used to stand for minutes at a time staring carefully and hopelessly in both directions, sure that the moment she stepped into the crosswalk a car would appear out of nowhere, racing at a hundred miles an hour to mow her down. She had imagined it vividly and repeatedly: the moment when, rooted to the spot by horror, she would be thrown under the wheels and dragged into bloody pulp.

In that case, of course, she would be unable to finish her novel.

Robin had said, "That's the craziest thing I've ever heard." But where had she gotten that paranoia from? That paralyzing fear that surfaced every time she took a risk, accepted a challenge, pushed herself to accomplish something?

Her father sneezed convulsively and blew his nose.

Some weed or other . . . it was getting on hayfever season . . . made him miserable his whole life, starting as a boy in the wheat fields . . . they'd had to send him home finally, useless and ashamed. If not for that, well, he might have been a farmer after all . . . it would have been a different life, healthier, not so sedentary. . . . His cousin, Jack, had the old farm now, back to see him once . . . at first he'd been excited to see everything as it had been, the swing in the tree, the barn in need of paint, horses like the one he used to ride . . .

but he and Jack had had nothing to say after the first hour. . . . "An accountant, eh, make a lot of money, eh, well, I see you've done well for yourself, Bob, eh?"

He and Nan had been out of place in their city clothes and shoes and Nan had embarrassed him by holding her nose in the yard . . . he'd left her with Jack's wife in the kitchen, hoping they would get along . . . but afterwards, driving back down the dirt road, Nan had joked about hayseeds, and "honestly, no one would ever suspect you came from that kind of background. . . ." But Polly had never minded, Polly had loved the country . . . it had been one of their plans to move back there one day, after the kids were grown, get a small place, a farm . . . it was Polly who had made it possible for him to marry a woman like Nan, a classy woman, a gourmet cook, a party-giver, a woman who had taste . . . and if she was a little high-strung and drank a little too much, well, that went along with it. . . .

Nan had found him on the floor that day . . . no, you couldn't ask for more in a woman . . . she'd brought him flowers every day and made sure the nurses took good care of him . . . and if occasionally she'd gotten on his nerves . . . she wanted him to get a hearing aid, but he was damned if he was going to accept it . . . how would it look to his clients? A hearing aid like some old fogey? He still had his pride, he was only sixty two, and if he was careful to get on the right side. . . .

Most people didn't move around as much as Kate. Or was she forgetting on purpose?

"Sorry, I said. . . ." She was conscious that she was shouting, and reduced herself to a gesture . . . this way was out. She'd completely forgotten about his hayfever . . . it was getting late anyway. Maybe they should be leaving soon. She thought of the relief it would be to get back to the motel and turn on the TV . . . let Nan take care of him . . . she knew how. . . .

But how could he have married her? That she could never

understand. "A man gets lonely," he'd said . . . and she knew what loneliness was, she expected to feel it her whole life. But Nan. "She's so different from Mom." "There's no one like your mother," he'd said simply. Still, getting married again meant he was forgetting her . . . forgetting Kate.

She followed him out of the herb garden, aimlessly, down a path trellised by roses. They had both lost their momentum . . . he seemed to have forgotten all about that lake, that house he'd been so excited about before. She looked at him from the back, trying to see him as just a man, a stranger, someone with no ties to herself. He still had a few photographs of himself growing up. She even remembered the stories that went along with them: the farm in Illinois, left to his cousin after his father died . . . a blond, thin boy on a horse . . . a photo of his mother and father's wedding . . . "Sixteen, she was only sixteen!" she'd cried out. "And I look like her." Dead at twenty in childbirth, her third child. His father was handsome, stiffly old-fashioned in the style of the times . . . a Scotch immigrant . . . too fragile-looking to have made a good farmer . . . "He tried hard, but he wore out, died at twenty-nine. . . ."

He hadn't had a scrapbook, not like the scrapbook her mother had kept of her and Kevin's baby pictures, family trips, birthdays and Christmases. His photos were few, stuffed into an old college yearbook, Illinois State . . . even then he'd looked reserved and important . . . a straight–A student and he'd held down a part-time job as well, no time for sports or fraternities. When she had stared into the tiny eyes of the yearbook's class photograph, she had seen that he was a hard worker, a survivor, someone who already knew that he had to get ahead or starve.

He took it all for granted. "Yes, I knew that life wasn't easy and that not everyone made it, and that some people fell by the wayside." Yes, he had actually used that phrase, "fell by the wayside." It had a fated, almost Biblical ring to it, she remembered. And she'd felt a strange chill, almost as if it were an accusation, a prophecy.

She and Kevin had always thought him so old-fashioned,

even as children . . . his fair, easily burned skin, the hayfever that kept him inside in summer, the suits he always wore, even around the house . . . he never played baseball with them or took them to the beach . . . but he had let her use his adding machine, had pulled out a book from the shelf called *Mein Kämpf* and told her its author was a "very bad man" . . . he came in his pajamas and got her when she'd screamed in the night, "There are bears in the closet," and he hadn't said no, but had carried her to the rocking chair and rocked and rocked her back to sleep.

"Daddy," she called softly up to him, trying out the word again.

His white head turned slightly, as if he strained to catch an unaccustomed tune.

The hearing played tricks as well as the mind. Just now he thought he'd heard Kate say, "Daddy" . . . a little girl trailing after him in a pink flowered dress . . . sometimes he thought it was coming back . . . the clear, piercing call of a bird at dawn . . . the threshing machines whirring in the fields of golden wheat . . . his mother calling out his name, "Robert, dinner!" . . . Jimmy Dorsey's singer, "You're a Lucky Guy" . . . then he would remember that those were old sounds, old words crackling in the left ear like a broken gramophone. . . . He'd told Nan once, "It's as if that ear is always listening to the past." "You should get a hearing aid," she'd told him.

"Daddy, Daddy." Kate would never call him that now . . . he had tried to be a good father, he just hadn't known how, he'd had no models . . . oh, it was easy when she and Kevin were little, so trusting . . . later he hadn't known what to say to them . . . "Your mother's dead" . . . he had done everything on his own, no parents to help him . . . what was a man supposed to do when his daughter moved in with some young fellow and then called him, crying, asking him to help her move? He really preferred not to know about Kate's life, it made him uncomfortable . . . it would have been so much simpler if she'd gotten married and had children . . . he liked being a grandfather to Kevin's kids, knew the exact relation he stood in in regards to them, Grandpa with the candy . . . but he always felt from Kate that she wanted something from him, he didn't know what . . . she refused to grow up, was that the problem? He didn't really know what she did, how she lived . . . oh, she said she was a coordinator, and she wrote . . . and she was probably involved with somebody or other . . . she had said long ago that she would never get married, didn't want to have children . . . but to continue to live with one man after another. . . .

And again he thought of the house by the lake, the wedding and Polly with her lilies . . . it had to be around here somewhere.

She composed words to his back: You never listened, you never knew what to say, you never cared. When you helped me pack up my things and drove me away to a friend's, you never said, "Why are you leaving him? What happened?" When I told you I was going away to forget you never asked, "Forget what?" You didn't tell me you were going to marry Nan. You never wanted to influence, be influenced. If I told you that I'd broken up again with someone, that I'd had an abortion because I was afraid of raising a child alone, afraid of how it would interfere with my life, you wouldn't know what to say. You never let us interfere with your life.

And yet she remembered the way he had held her as a child, had held Kevin's babies, the way he had taken her cat from her when she left and talked to it and scratched its ears.

He kept his head cocked now, always . . . made him look curiously alert, yet dreamy . . . he must think of the past, of his life, wonder what it had all meant, losing so many people who had been important to him, those who had influenced him . . . and there it was again . . . she had simply not been important to him once she grew up. It was futile to . . . but he was moving quickly now, striding down the path with unusual eagerness.

"What's the hurry?" she called. He didn't hear her . . .

she had forgotten about the house . . . and yet there, in a minute, it stood, exactly as he'd described it, "a Victorian house
by a small lake" . . . and he was climbing its porch and looking in all its windows like a boy of six.

What satisfaction . . . that one thing from the past still
remained intact, exactly the same . . . he turned to Kate and
for an instant was checked . . . where were her pink flowered
dress, her glossy brown curls, her trilling, childish voice?
Thin, anxious-looking, she watched, as a mother might watch
a child, fearful that he would fall, afraid to say anything.

"Your mother," he said, hardly conscious that he spoke,
unable to hear himself, "lived in a house like this. We were
married there."

She opened her mouth, but no sound came out.

The Hulk

"If you have a color TV it's even better," Nina says. "He's green."

"I'm glad Lisa doesn't," I respond with some feeling. "This is bad enough. That guy has too many muscles for his own good. It's not healthy."

"You intellectuals," she scoffs. "I bet you don't even have a TV."

It's true, but I don't tell her that. I've never liked being called an intellectual. Hell, I never finished college and I'm starving on food stamps. What's so smart about that?

"Ooo, there he goes," she says excitedly. "He's turning into the Hulk. He can't help himself."

I stare at her in real amazement. She's not kidding, she is truly thrilled and stimulated by his transformation from ordinary guy to raving maniac. In spite of having spent the last four days in her company I wouldn't have believed it.

But then, I don't know her at all. It's been one of those awkward situations where you're mad at your lover and want to get away, so you think of your old friend Lisa who says please come to L.A., I'd love to see you, and then she turns out to be having a desperate and passionate affair with someone you never meet and meanwhile some other acquaintance is crashing in her apartment. So it ends up not really a visit to anyone, just a kind of protracted limbo in the company of somebody you don't know and probably don't like and it's three days before Christmas, your lover is calling you collect begging you to come back and here's this guy foaming at the fangs, two stories tall, with a torso like sixteen tightly rolled sleeping bags lashed together, throwing people out the window.

"Ooo, ooo," says Nina; "oh, ouch." Then, seriously to me, "The really tragic part about it is that he doesn't like doing these things. He's always remorseful and they're looking for some way to cure him. It's like a parable of mankind, you know?"

In spite of both direct and round about questions I have not yet been able to discover what Nina usually does, or how she makes a living or any of the normal things you might want to know about a person you're ending up having to depend upon for complete emotional support. She isn't young, I know that. Her hair is going gray and it's permanented into curls that she heaps forward on her crown like a 1940's comedienne (though it may be the latest style for all I know). About thirty-five, I'd say, maybe older; indifferent about dress, usually wearing voluminous pants and a tube top that flattens her large breasts like an ace bandage. She has spidery long fingers and feet the same, a round kind of face devoid of expressions but not of mystery. In fact, I find her extremely mysterious, though somehow familiar looking. Where did she come from? How did Lisa meet her? What is she doing staying here?

I haven't had a chance to pose these questions to Lisa. In with a hug, out with a kiss, meanwhile changing her clothes and ruffling through the bills.

"Heard from A.J. yet?" she asks. Her large brown eyes regard me with what momentarily appears to be concern.

"Four times in the last two days. She doesn't want to talk about it on the phone, all she wants is for me to come back. *Then* we'll talk about it, she says, but I know that once I go back. . . .''

''Give her my love,'' Lisa smiles warmly, vaguely, and then: ''Gotta run, *he*'s waiting.''

Lisa, my dearest high school friend, how can you do this to me? Remember the locker we shared, the little notes you wrote me with *x*'s at the bottom for smooches, how your mother let me run away to your house when things got bad at home? And how we've kept in touch all these years, over ten years, in spite of living in different cities and you being a successful screen writer and me just a hopeful nothing. It was you I came down to see, I even thought that maybe . . . but no, *he*'s waiting. Christ, in the eleventh grade you would have been ashamed of yourself.

''Have you ever met this, uh, friend of Lisa's?'' I ask Nina.

She is reading the huge bulk of the *L. A. Times,* inch by column inch, with close-up concentration.

''Nnnn,'' she says.

I think, she can't be as stupid as she seems if she reads the paper so thoroughly. I try, ''What's your opinion on the hostages?''

''Uhhnnn,'' she says.

I leave her. It's not like I have nothing to do. I brought five books with me to read and a notebook to fill up and a short story or two to work on. It's not like I have to sit around making conversation with this woman or wait for Lisa to turn up or A. J. to call again. I have my fucking life to figure out!

I write in my notebook. I pace the floor. I go out, down to the Mexican restaurant at the bottom of the hill, along Sunset visiting the Cuban grocery for a mango ice. I come back and sit in the garden with Volume Three of Virginia Woolf's *Letters* and stare out through raggedy palms at the Hollywood Freeway. I hate being alone but I can't concentrate (I tell myself) with Nina always around.

She never goes anywhere.

First she gets up and reads the paper. This takes about two hours. Then she washes her hair and works on her curls with an electric wand. Then she lies, fully dressed, in the sun for a while and finally puts on a record, does a few exercises and settles down to watch TV. She doesn't do dishes because she never cooks. She eats sunflower seeds and fruit and drinks kefir out of the carton. She is actually very tidy. All her possessions are in one box; she never takes them out for long, simply rearranges them when she finishes her toilette. She sleeps on top of Lisa's bed in a sleeping bag. . . .

But I'm making it sound as if we don't talk at all, when, in truth, we have exchanged some bits of conversation. Not about the hostages or Lisa's hot stuff or my worries or hers, if she has any, but strange pieces of dialogue—meaningful, if you could understand them.

For instance, yesterday she says to me, "Do you think the world is going to end pretty soon or not?"

Astonished, all I can mutter is, "I don't know."

"I hope it doesn't," she says, and a faint blush of sadness slips across her round face, so unwrinkled, so incongruous under the pile-up of graying curls.

It makes me feel sad too. All this quarreling and feeling and hoping for nothing. So I say gently and with sympathy, "Don't worry about it. No use worrying about it."

"Oh, but I have to," she says earnestly. "I'm thinking of going to Santa Fe, you know."

Confused, I think she means she knows of some top-secret bunker there where she can hide from the nuclear destruction. I want to ask her if she'll give me the address, but suddenly she says, quite cheerfully, "Santa Fe's a nice place. It's hot there."

Most of our conversations take place, not during commercials, as you would expect, for then Nina sits rapt and solemn, watching the antics of flying candy bars and yodeling housewives, but during the shows themselves, when she is moved to offer some comment about the nature of the universe as expressed through a sit-com or adventure.

She laughs, she oohs, she groans, her normally expressionless face becomes animated; she turns to me and says thoughtfully, "Do you believe in good and evil?"

"Just evil."

"Oh, I think there's always room for improvement," she says seriously.

And so we are sitting watching the Hulk, now a regular chump again and indeed full of remorse at having been pushed too far and gone large and destructive, when the phone rings.

I answer it, prepared for the operator.

"Will you accept a collect call from Alice Jones?"

"Go ahead," I sigh. "Well, what now?"

"Oh Cary, I miss you so much. When are you coming back?"

"I'm not coming back until you get your head examined."

"But that will take too long. You have to come back before then. The cats miss you. Fred isn't eating his kibble."

I steel my heart. Poor Fred. "There's no use us discussing this, A.J. I'm prepared to make changes. But you have to make them too."

"What changes?" she says eagerly, as if the subject had never been broached before.

"You know what changes." I'm starting to get worked up. "I've told you over and over that I can't stand you shouting at me and calling me names. Then claiming you had a nervous breakdown and don't remember anything."

"What names? Cary, I never call you names."

"What do you think egotist is then?"

"It's not a name. It's a description."

"Description of you, you mean. I'm perfectly happy working and writing by myself. I don't need your compan-ionship day and night. I don't need someone to pay attention to me all the time."

"You don't love me," she chokes. "That's it, isn't it?"

"Oh Christ." I slam the phone down and tell it, "And don't call me anymore either."

Nina's eyes are devouring a disembodied hand rolling two different kinds of anti-perspirant across a piece of glass. I stare bitterly at her shoulders emerging from the tube top. She has beautiful skin, but not so beautiful as A.J.'s dancer's silk.

"Is he going to turn into the Hulk again?" I try moodily, but not without some desire for reassurance.

"Nnnn," she says. "He only does it once a show."

"I've got to know, who is she?" I whisper the next morning, following Lisa out the front door. She's been here five minutes, long enough to grab a notebook and put on a clean shirt.

"Oh, Nina? She's just somebody I know."

"From where? A trip to the moon, maybe?"

"She is kind of spacey, isn't she? You'd never guess she was a pretty well-known TV actress as a kid, would you?"

"Lisa! You're shitting me."

We are almost to the car where *he* is waiting. I can barely make him out behind the wheel, can only see that he has large hairy hands and sunglasses. The early morning sunshine suddenly strikes me in the pit of my stomach.

"I don't know the whole story," Lisa says absently, her brown eyes glowing at the sight of him. "Something about she was going to get her own serial and her husband threw her out or maybe he beat her, I forget . . . I met her at Sally's. . . . We'll all have to get together for dinner one of these times."

"When?" I'm desperate, want to hang on to her, drag her back inside.

"Oh, *soon*," Lisa says brightly and pops into the car.

In the living room Nina is doing her spidery long nails over in a thick and plummy lacquer. She waves them about while she studies the business pages. Her face, as usual, reveals nothing, though now that I know she was—is—an actress she looks both more interesting and more beautiful. I try to think what show I could have seen her in as a child— *Wagon Train? Father Knows Best? Leave It to Beaver?* . . . and I am suddenly, and uncomfortably, aware of her large breasts; unrestrained for the first time by the tube top, they hang like twin eggplants, meaty but with a thin, satin finish, under a loose, unbuttoned shirt.

Has someone hurt you? I feel like asking. Or, Do you think people are responsible for everything they say? Did he really hit you? Oh, look at me. What happened to you?

"Lisa tells me you're interested in acting. . . ."

She doesn't even glance up. "Uhhnnn."

I think of writing a story about A.J. except I remember how she screamed at me, "You fuckin' egotist and now you'll probably put that in a story too." It's not worth fictionalizing, she's not worth it, but all the same I wonder if I could get into words what I used to feel about her and how it changed. How her anger changed everything.

At first I was amazed and guilty. What had I said, what had I done to make her lash out like that? I would stand in a freezing sweat watching her face thicken up and her words gnash out, "You always," "You never," "You can't do this to me." Going for the throat, the most wounding phrase. "You bitch, I'm sick of your smartass shit. You think you're so great, you can't even get a grant."

She could get mad at me for anything, and it would be over as soon as it came out. "Oh Cary, I'm sorry. I don't know what came over me. I don't even remember what I said."

She would be refreshed, happy as a little buddha. When I would try, in my torturously painful fashion, to reason through her feelings: "Are you angry because I have to spend a lot of time alone? I know it doesn't seem like working to you, I know it doesn't bring in much money . . . I don't mean to be selfish. . . ."

"Oh Cary, I understand. I really do. You're going to be a great writer someday and I want to help you."

"But you just said. . . ."

"Oh, don't think about that. I'm just feeling a little crazy today. It's my period." Or "my job." Or "my parents." Or almost anything.

If I continued to press ahead with my guilt and desire to

do right by her, she would burst into tears. "Oh, I'm so worthless, I'm so unhappy, I don't know what I want to do, I had a terrible day at work."

The sight of her tears always made me remorseful, eager to comfort. It was my fault that she stopped being a dancer and became a bus driver. And god knows, nobody's life was easy, everybody could break down sometimes with tension, look for someone to blame. . . .

But I learned one thing pretty quickly and that was not to cry in front of her myself. Both times I did, driven by complete despair, I watched her eyes widen with victory, with delight. She didn't come over and take me by the shoulders, whisper that it was all right, that she loved me. She only smiled greedily and went in for the kill.

If I was strong she respected me. If I was weak, so much the worse.

The only solution was to keep silent, to let her blow herself out. But who could go on like that forever? We went on for five years.

Lisa turns up on Christmas Eve, quiet and carrying two bags of groceries.

"He's eating with his family," she announces. "I thought we could do something with a ham."

Certainly Lisa feels abandoned, but after an hour or so she regains her cheerfulness, cutting up vegetables, boiling potatoes, stirring up an eggnog batter. Besides, she's going to sleep with *him* tonight. It's not so far away.

We drink some eggnog, even Nina, and suddenly nothing is quite so bad, it's Christmas after all, and Lisa is brilliantly reminiscent, "Remember that turkey Mr. Harris and his toupee in French class?"

"Oh, Jean-Jacques Rousseau, and his slides of sailors in Marseilles." We grow hysterical. "Remember, remember?" I think I haven't been so happy in a long time. Lisa is all shining brown eyes and peachy mouth and I remember the first time we kissed, and she says, "If only you weren't so moral about writing for the movies.''

I don't get insulted at all. ''Oh, I don't know. I think I could write a pretty good script for the Hulk.''

''The Hulk!'' she shrieks. ''Oh my god, have you been watching that? Isn't that the trashiest thing?''

''I like it,'' Nina speaks up.

''It's like a parable of mankind,'' I hoot.

''That's right,'' she smiles, and for the first time I think, I *do* like her and she likes me.

''You two,'' sighs Lisa.

We beam all around, but just then the telephone rings. It's bound to be the Hulk, so I get up and answer it. No, it's *him,* unable to make it through a single evening without Lisa. Strangely enough I am jealous handing the receiver to her, watching her face go dreamy and expectant.

They murmur back and forth. I hear her whisper, ''I miss you,'' and, ''Yes, in an hour,'' and my pleasure vanishes.

I'm simply a bit drunk and more than a little unhappy. What can A.J. be doing tonight? Is she alone, does she miss me? Or is she out with someone I might not even know, is she thinking of going to bed with her? Has she given up on me completely?

''More eggnog?'' says Lisa.

I think I could actually jump up and start screaming at her.

Now it's later and she's gone to fuck and be fucked. Nina and I sit in front of the television, watching a special. But even she doesn't have her heart in it. When the phone rings she jumps up as if it's for her, and it is.

''Hello. Yes, hello. Yes, fine.''

I try not to listen. Her husband, mother, children?

''No, nothing.''

''Uhhh.''

''No, I can't. . . . How are. . . .''

She gives me a quick glance, half turns away. Where have I seen her before? I go into the bathroom and think about my

Hulk script.

It could begin as a sit-com: two roommates (of course you don't say they're gay), both *artistes.* One gives up dancing and finds a job as a bus driver because she doesn't want to be poor. The other struggles through low-paying part-time jobs and writes, and never worries about money and is happy when she isn't feeling guilty. It's sort of like the Odd Couple. The writer is at home, either forgetting to wash the dishes or cleaning everything up in a frenzy of neatness (both connected with writing). The other is angry about having to go to work all day and comes home. . . .

Suddenly turns into the Hulk, breaks the dishes, throws the writer's typewriter in the trashcan and. . . .

Suddenly it doesn't seem so funny.

Nina is off the phone when I come out, with no expression on her face to show what has passed. However, she is drinking rum straight out of the bottle, a bad sign.

Naturally, I join her.

We sit in front of the TV with the sound turned down on some people singing carols.

"So, when are you going to Tucson?" I ask.

"I'm not going anywhere." Nina regards me with equanimity and, I notice abruptly, a little something extra. Interest? Sexual interest? The tentative beginnings of lust? I hope it's not just my imagination, but something seems to have opened up between us, something warm and zippy. *Rawhide?* I wonder. *The Donna Reed Show?* The line of her tube top is low on her chest, the cleavage deep and swelling. I begin to have terrible fantasies of pulling it down, just to see the way the lovely eggplants would pop out.

The Hulk is a monster in all of us, I think solemnly. I could want to turn into a beastly thing, grow two stories high and carry her off to bed.

Of course it all turns out much differently. I don't think I could ravish someone if I tried, and I am back to wondering, *The Ozzie and Harriet Show? Bonanza?* when she says calmly, looking me straight in the eye, "Want to go to bed?"

It isn't, all expectations and rum to the contrary, completely satisfactory. Nina's response to passion seems to consist only of gripping my head between her legs and muttering, "Go on, go *on.*"

I *am* going on, at least as best I can under conditions of extreme claustrophobia. I try to imagine myself in a nice hot place, inside an oven with a loaf of baking bread. Bread, yes, Nina is like a soft, spongy loaf, from the sweet dough of her bumpy thighs to her yeasty stomach. She is also, in spite of my best efforts, as dry and hot as unbuttered toast down there. For some reason I keep recalling that Nina was famous once and I saw her, I watched her on TV, and this upsets me. I mean, not knowing for sure, which show. It's not really that much of a turn-on for me to make love with someone I know nothing about.

At least part of me feels that. The other part is longing desperately for A.J., for her mossy pebble in its spring-fed pool. For the first time I truly understand the meaning of the term "dry as a bone." Nina's cunt is arid as a tiny desert and it's sucking the saliva right out of my mouth without leaving a coating.

"Go on," she clamors, but her tone is hardly aroused, much less arousing. She sounds, instead, embarrassed. I raise my head and stare at her. She's not sweating but a kind of sunlamp heat seems to radiate off her body. It's cooking me too.

"Are you all right?" I whisper dryly.

She opens her eyes and I see how dilated the pupils are and, slow as I am, it occurs to me that Nina must be drugged. All child stars turn into drug addicts, you know. Immediately several things become clear, her drifting gaze, her sluggish responses, even her occasional manic energy while watching TV and the slightly philosophic bent of her thoughts.

But even as I stare at her, horrified, her pupils seem to contract into something like a normal look, half shy, half despairing, and when she speaks her voice is perfectly calm: "I guess I can't come."

I sort of roll off then into Lisa's pillows.

"My husband always told me I was a lesbian, and I always wondered, but I guess I'm not."

Faint groan from me, disguised as a cough.

"Are you mad?" she asks.

I recover my voice. "No, I'm not mad." But even to my own ears I sound that way: disgruntled, angry, disappointed. How can I explain that that's how I'm feeling about myself this minute?

"You don't have to perform for me," I tell her. "I'm not a man."

"Maybe if we just lie here," she says hopelessly.

It's the last thing I want to do. My heart is crippled with sadness and desire for A.J. It's all I can do not to jump up and try and call her. But I don't. It would only be the same if I went back, I know that now more than ever somehow. So we lie here, side by side, not touching, until Nina asks,

"Have you ever been hit?"

I shake my head. "No, just words."

"Oh, words," she says, vehement. "I hate words too. But when it turns into hitting, that's the worst."

I don't even need to ask, do you want to talk about it, because the story comes spilling out. It's an old story and a new one and it gives me the creeps because it's so much like my own. Nina's husband only hit her a couple of times (only) but he spent a lot of time telling her he was going to. He had been a child star too, in the same serial (that famous one, now I remember, *Dad's Kids*) and he'd gone on acting for a while, though he never got very good parts. He'd wanted Nina to stay home and have children and she couldn't and after a few years he'd gone into real estate and she'd started drinking and then she'd stopped and she'd tried to get some acting jobs and had been offered one and that was when the violence began.

All the time she's telling me this I'm remembering more and more clearly the cute little teenage brother and sister on the show and how I loved them, Cathy and Bob. And I'm remembering that the first time A.J. really screamed at me was when I had a story published in a good magazine and

how guilty I felt, knowing she had given up, and suddenly
Nina and I are clinging together, crying as if our hearts would
break.

That seems to damp everything down and when we try
again to make love it's wet and thick and warm as a beach
towel drying in the sun, half soft, half rough and completely
comfortable.

The next morning, Christmas morning, is very eventful.
First Lisa comes breezing in with *him,* Rodney, "call me
Rod," and proceeds to make breakfast for him.

"There was nothing at *his* house," she explain breezily,
tunneling back into the refrigerator past Nina's kefir and my
stale tortillas to the ham, and leaving me and Nina to make
conversation with him.

We discuss Jerry Brown and the hostages and he has a lot
of opinions as befits an up-and-coming screen writer. He is
also very hairy, and it's not just his hands but large areas of
his body: chest, arms, legs (all uncovered, this is L. A.). I take
a deeper dislike to him and so does Nina when he suddenly
says, "Say, weren't you little teenage Cathy in *Dad's Kids?*"

"Uhhnnn," she says.

Unlike me he is persistent. "Well, weren't you?"

Fortunately Lisa calls out, "Come and get it," and, not
mistaking the invitation to include us, Nina and I slink off to
the bedroom. I feel very much in love with her this morning
and pull down her tube top less with beastliness than with
the desire for reassurance that those satiny eggplants are still
there.

When we come out again Lisa and *he* (I mean, *Rod*) are
having an argument, their first, to judge by Lisa's alarmed
looks. It has something to do with the screenplay they are
writing together.

"Women don't talk like that," she is trying to reason.

"What do you know about it? My first wife used to talk
exactly like that." He looks at us unpleasantly. "Ask little
Cathy, she used to talk like that too. 'I'm so proud of you,

Daddy' and she's thinking 'Go fuck yourself, Daddy.' "

"Go fuck yourself, *Rod,*" little Cathy says calmly.

This enrages *him* even more, the sight and sound of all these women who are not talking like they're supposed to, and he snarls, "Say, Lisa, who are these girls anyway? What are they doing here? Is that why you haven't wanted me to come over? What are they, your dyke friends or something?"

I would like to be able to report that the three of us, Lisa included, turn into Hulks, or better, the Furies, right then and pummel him to supertenderized beef, but instead we just stand there, embarrassed, and hot and hairy Rod seems to realize that even without lifting a finger towards him we are all just too much and stalks out the door. And I would like also to be able to say that Lisa shrugs her shoulders and goes back to writing the first feminist car-crash epic by herself, but instead she lights out after him with scarcely a look at us. And a minute later we hear the car zoom off.

The second thing that happens this morning, just as Nina and I are getting comfortable in bed together, is that the doorbell rings and it's the other *him*, Nina's husband, aka little Bob, the innocently sexy, wimp-curled boy who once threw me into a frenzy of desire at ten. Needless to say he's quite changed by now, though he still looks younger than Nina. He too is extremely hairy and (dare I say it?) rather Hulk-like.

He says more or less the same things as Rod but they're all directed at me (it's true my zipper turns out to be undone): "Who is she? She looks like a dyke." Etc. I find I am getting tired of this. I mean, what is this radar they have? My own aunt, the noted spiritualist, doesn't have a clue. And I say, borrowing little Cathy's secret lines, "Fuck off."

Never did I suspect what a powerful phrase this is. First *him*, then *him*, both turned away by those magic words. I wonder why I never used them on A.J.

So little Bob leaves too (with a little additional encouragement from Nina, who stoically claims she will call the police) and right then the third thing happens.

A.J. walks in the door.

"Cary," she says, tearful and carrying her suitcase, deter-

mined not to notice the former child star cursing and stomp-
ing past her, "I had to come."

"Nina," I say. "The Hulk."

Then I have to sit down. It's been a hectic day (Christmas,
what Christmas?) and I know that nothing is going to drive
A.J. away, short of a complete confession, and maybe not
even that.

"Uhhnnn," says Nina. "Hi." And gives me a piercing
look before retiring to the bathroom.

A.J. doesn't even ask who she is. "I just flew here on the
spur of the minute. I had such an awful time last night. I
couldn't stand to be alone."

If only she were angry; I could deal with her like the men
who'd just passed through the living room. But instead she's
in one of her most abject and frightened moods. She's going
to go through with the scene whether I want to or not. All I
can do is get her outside, into the little plot of garden overlooking the Hollywood Freeway. It's not that I don't love her;
yes, I do, and she looks better than ever, with her dancer's
strong and graceful limbs, her perfectly symmetrical fea-
tures. You wouldn't guess to look at her that that face could
ever harden up like wall spackle in a mask of complete
hatred and comtempt. You wouldn't guess that this sweet
and loving voice, saying, "Cary, Cary, how I've missed you,"
could ever say, "I hate you, you bitch."

"Well, aren't you glad to see me?" she asks, as we stand
watching the lovely vision of an almost empty freeway on
Christmas morning while the sun shines down out of a clear
and hardly smoggy sky. "I've come all this way to tell you
I'm sorry, I'm really sorry, and I need you back."

I'm touched. Who wouldn't be? But it's somehow no
longer enough. Even the thought of her little frolicking, moss-
covered pebble is no longer enough.

So I just say, "Uhhnnn."

Naturally A.J. didn't give up easily. There was plenty to
promise—a new schedule, she'd get back to dancing, damn

the money, do what she really wanted, we'd been happier then, it was important that I keep writing, she wouldn't call me names, she'd *understand*, and she did understand. . . . And plenty to reproach me with—my egotism, my indifference, all she'd given up for me, how I took everything so seriously, our five years together, she never thought I'd leave her. Eventually she found out (I told her, I mean) that I'd slept with Nina (once so far) and all hell broke loose—I was a traitor, a liar, what did I see in her, Nina was a jerk, had been terrible as little Cathy, was old now and could hardly put a sentence together.

She stayed two days, yelled half the time and cried the other half, while Lisa called to ask how long I'd be staying (not that she wanted to drive me out because we were really such good friends, remember that French class, but *he* was just wondering), and while Nina quietly made reservations for Santa Fe. For two.

And when A.J. finally left, we left too, if not to find a place where the world wouldn't end, then to protect ourselves a little from people who wanted to destroy us, and, maybe, to prevent ourselves from turning into Hulks too.

We're still here. Lisa writes us sometimes—she's still with *him* and claims she's unhappy, without seeing any way out— but as Nina was saying the other day backstage at the Santa Fe Women's Theater (I wrote the play, she's starring), there's always room for improvement.

Miss Venezuela

There was a boardwalk once, surfacing through the sand only to disappear if you tried to follow it. Gray rough timber made porous by the salt air, it was hotter than ordinary wood, much hotter, Rhonda and Eric agreed, jumping on and off with tender young feet, and screaming loudly if they caught a splinter.

The boardwalk belonged to an earlier time; if you looked up at the mural over the entrance to the Long Beach Municipal Auditorium, you could puzzle out which era—unless you were a child, that is, and could ask your mother everything.

"Why are those girls wearing shorts in the water?"

"They're not shorts, they're bathing costumes."

"They're funny," said Eric, but Rhonda always looked and wondered. She liked the mural very much; it was faded but still colorful, like an old advertisement painted on a barn. It depicted a crowded seaside scene, all blues and yellows. Two young women with strong thighs and muscular arms disported in the shallow waves. Their hair was clipped around smiling faces and the costumes were sheer and black, looking painted on, as indeed they were.

"Bathing beauties," said Helen, their mother, and laughed a little, possibly because neither woman was particularly beautiful.

That was left to a few gorgeous creatures in the background who waved parasols with bamboo handles and Chinese fans against the summer heat. Modishly wasp-waisted and refined from every angle, the women still looked pale and droopy to Rhonda compared with the frolicking swimmers in the water.

"I bet the ones in the long dresses wish they could take everything off and go in the water," she observed once.

"Oh, I doubt it," said Helen.

"But they're not going to have any fun like that."

"Beauty never does," sniffed her mother. "That's not what it's there for."

———— • ————

Dolores María Angelus Otero was born in Caracas in 1940. Her father, Rafael Otero, was a *mestizo* from the Sierra Nevada de Mérida. For helping to organize a student strike he had been exiled with hundreds of others in 1928 under the dictatorship of Juan Vicente Gómez. He fled to Costa Rica, where he married the daughter of a butcher, Eva López Angelus. The two of them, with Eva pregnant, returned to Caracas in 1940. There they worked with Rómulo Betancourt and Acción Democrática until 1948, when Major Marco Pérez Jiménez brutally took power. Rafael Otero was jailed for the political crime of trade unionism and sent to the infamous Guasina Island camp in the jungles of Orinoco. He may have been tortured to death, though the certificate read that malaria was the cause.

Dolores Otero grew up after 1948 in a squatter's shack on the hills around the capital. They had a dirt floor and no running water, but Dolores had a good education. Her mother read her the novels of Gallegos, the poetry of Martí and Darío and Neruda, and gave her the oral history of resistance in Venezuela, starting with Simón Bolívar, the Great Liberator. Eva told her daughter that when Betancourt came to power again the foreign oil companies would pay for what they had done to Venezuela. Meanwhile, in Cuba, a group of bearded men and brave women were fighting in the Sierra Maestra against their dictator. Eva, though not Dolores (who was by this time attending the university), was among the crowd that stoned Richard Nixon, American vice-president, in 1958, during his visit to Caracas.

Eva died shortly after, of tuberculosis, ironically just months before Pérez Jiménez was driven from office and Betancourt, her old friend from exile and Acción Democrática, formed a new, democratic régime.

Dolores had no brothers or sisters, and only a few relatives she had never met in Mérida and Costa Rica. She was a brilliant and independent girl, however, strikingly beautiful and something of a troublemaker. She wanted both to make a lot of money and to change the world. She was also fatally unsophisticated, and before she was nineteen had had two abortions and had lost her place at the university.

———•———

Near the Municipal Auditorium there was a long pier, where you could walk out and have clam chowder or fritters or buy abalone ashtrays or shell-studded box purses. It was lined with people in windbreakers, fishing, hooking their lines with raw bait from a tin bucket and catching tires and bottles and sometimes sea bass. There was a smell of oil and tar, a tang so fierce and fresh it almost burned. Sunsets, seen from the pier, were orange and red in winter, pastel in summer. And sometimes you could see Catalina Island, a low dinosaur on the horizon. There were no large waves anymore, though Long Beach was once known for its surf. The word "breakwater" used to confuse Rhonda, for how could water break?

The ocean water was always a little dirty and hardworking from the port and the navy base, and full of bits of wood and big kelp bubbles. Rhonda and Eric, with Helen watching from the shore, still swam and bobbled in it, talking about sharks to scare each other, but never seeing any, seeing only jellyfish, rounds of white transparency, like slices of albino fruit. At intervals along the shore, as they walked back to the car, were the longlegged lifeguard stations, chapped by the wind and deserted in winter.

There was the Pike, before they cleaned it up, when it was still adult and rough and smacking of war. In later years Rhonda and Eric would dare each other to go there, among the tatoo-parlors and the blood banks and the side shows of freaks and animals and the fun houses, among the pawn shops and cardhalls and shops selling souvenirs for wives and girlfriends of the sailors, to the rickety calligraphy of the roller coaster, the one they said threw people off into the ocean as if they were dead fleas flying from the coat of a running dog.

Helen and Bob, their parents, had met at the Pike during a wartime dance, but they avoided the place now. Helen explained that the water in the pool called The Plunge was half pee and half spittle. And as Helen and Bob were themselves moving up in the world, so they all moved up geographically from the low life of the pier and the Pike to the fresh glamour of the bluff and Ocean Boulevard, with its divider of green grass, tall palms, its half-timbered mansions interspersed with neat little pink and yellow hotels called SeaView and Ocean Breeze.

They moved up to the Pacific Coast Club.

———————•———————

Dolores's first lover was the son of an oilman. Eva would have been shocked if she had known. Ever since the oil deposits had been discovered in the Lake Maracaibo basin and Gómez had awarded lucrative contracts to foreign developers, Venezuela had been in the hands of Gulf, Standard Oil and Royal Dutch Shell. The native Venezuelans who embezzled with them grew rich too, built villas around Caracas and vacationed in Europe on the graft money. Hermann's father was white, a *caudillo* turned businessman who had gone to Yale and who knew the Rockefellers intimately. Hermann had grown up mostly in New York, attending private schools, and had spent his summers in Maine and his winters in Switzerland.

To be honest, Hermann was not as bad as he might have been. A short, rather serious boy, he was too romantic, too generous, to be a good playboy. He was genuinely intrigued by Dolores, whose rich dark beauty had attracted him from a chauffeured car on a Caracas street. He was only eighteen, a year older than Dolores, and this was his first real foray into Venezuelan life. The fact that Dolores's father had been a member of the Generation of '28 and that he had been persecuted by Pérez Jiménez, the same man who had helped make his father rich, gave her additional glamour in his eyes. Without the knowledge of his family, he arranged meetings with her in a highrise apartment building and began to tutor her in the ways of the wealthy.

Dolores took to the life immediately. She was old enough to have a contempt for everything Hermann represented and young enough to long for it desperately. While arguing politics with him she consumed four-course meals; with money discreetly left in a drawer she bought clothes and took English lessons. To assuage her guilt she also bought presents for her classmates and handed out dozens of bolivars every day to beggars.

In the end she grew fond of Hermann who, after all, was always so kind to her. When she became pregnant, Hermann said he would go to his father and ask to marry her. That was the last she ever saw of Hermann. A woman who said she was his mother came to the luxury apartment, welcomed Dolores into the family and said she was taking her to the doctor for a check-up. Under anesthesia, the baby was aborted. When Dolores woke up she was in a dark room and bleeding. Hermann's mother was gone. Her own mother she never told.

Dolores was more careful with her next lover, a businessman who traveled frequently. She continued attending the university and decided on a career in law. She did not live with Ricardo, even after her mother died, but she accepted willingly his gifts and dinners. When she became pregnant again she knew what to do and did it. But something changed inside her after that: there were complications, an infection set in, and when it was cured, the doctor said she was sterile.

It was 1959 and Castro and his fellow revolutionaries had just overthrown Batista, but Dolores's university career was cut short by her inability to explain her long absence from class.

———————•———————

The Pacific Coast Club was a brown sandcastle of rather fantastic appearance, built on the side of a bluff. It had a turret, stained glass windows, a red carpet leading from the sidewalk through the gold-leafed doors and a lobby complete with doorman, leather book to sign in and huge fireplace. Off the lobby was a patio restaurant, with a marble pond owned by three very large old carp and supervised by waiters in white jackets who didn't like children.

Though the lobby was plush with old leather and humidors, the beach at the base of the club was strictly tropical. A bamboo fence surrounded it; there was an outdoor cafe where people in bright sarongs and polo shirts sipped tall pink and orange drinks. There were umbrellas and striped lounge chairs laid out in rows. Here you could see older women the color of walnuts and oily as fish lying hour after hour in their bikinis, with two little white half eggs shielding their eyes.

Although they, Bob, Helen, Rhonda and Eric, passed through this private beach on their way to the ocean, it wasn't a place any of them lingered in, any more than they did the lobby.

"Too fancy," sturdy Helen said, while privately yearning. Both Helen and Bob were nondrinkers as well as a little pale and stout. They looked best in their roles as Mother and

Father, and sought out those like themselves at the club, rather than the heirs to oil fortunes and orange groves around Disneyland.

No, their sphere was the level in between lobby and beach, the physical family world of the Ladies' and Men's Locker Rooms, pool and gym. The pool, Olympic-sized, was ostensibly the reason for joining the club in the first place. Helen and Bob, who were bringing up their children in California as if it were their own Midwest, on canned vegetables, snowflecked Christmas trees and tales of hardship, religion and struggle, nevertheless insisted early that their children learn to swim—not as they had, fearfully dipping and plunging in summer waterholes and rivers, or later, by the shores of Lake Michigan, learning the awkward, head-elevated breaststroke—but really learn to swim. This did not mean an occasional dip in the urinated, snotty waters of Pike's Plunge, but special swimsuits and classes—beginner, intermediate, advanced—and for Rhonda, finally, the swim team. It meant that Saturdays were swim days at the club—eyes smarting from chlorine, ears clogged and muscles pleasantly heavy. It meant, eventually, dozens of boring laps, swim meets with whistles blowing and terrifying views from the high dive. But it also meant, always, the Ladies' Locker Room.

———•———

Dolores Otero had both a common and a distinctive beauty. She was on the short side, with large breasts and a nipped-in, curvaceous figure. Slightly bowed legs only gave her a more provocative stance, as she habitually leaned on one hip to compensate. Her hair was black, her skin was gold. All this was attractive and very Venezuelan. Where she differed was in the high cheekbones and the great Egyptian eyes, accented with a curling wave of eyeliner. Her nose was straight and delicate; her lips formed a naturally red ridge over small white teeth.

"Elegant, but sexy," approved several judges.

"Nefertiti," said another.

Dolores, in the course of looking up a professor who she hoped would intercede for her in the matter of her dismissal, had wandered into a beauty contest.

The ten other young women, one of whom, an almost natural blonde, had thought she had it in the bag, watched carefully as Dolores sauntered through the room.

"They told me Professor Carlos Guerrera was here?"

"Name?"

"Dolores María Angelus Otero . . . have I made a mistake?"

"Not the daughter of Rafael?" exclaimed one man, jumping up to embrace her. "We were in Costa Rica together. And Eva?"

"Eva's dead. . . ."

Such sympathy in the room. Daughter of a hero—in '59 you could say it—a distinctive Venezuelan beauty—an orphan now. All at once the men began to explain the advantages of being Miss Venezuela. The money, the chance to travel, the opportunity to represent the new democratic Venezuelan state to the world. She was a patriot certainly, the daughter of Rafael couldn't be anything else. But it was the promise of a scholarship that swayed Dolores most. For if she had a scholarship, surely she would be able to return to law school.

———————•———————

To Rhonda, at seven, the Ladies' Locker Room was huge, as big as an underground city, with streets and avenues of tiny rooms, cubicles for dressing and undressing, each one with a shower and six lockers. The ceiling was high, though the walls dividing the rooms were low; the floor was entirely cement, drained at intervals by sieved holes. There were no doors, only white cloth curtains that never quite closed.

The Ladies' Locker Room had a very special smell, the combination of ripe femaleness and water. It was the odor of women undressing in small spaces, struggling with their girdles and stiff brassieres, panting a little, giving off eddies of perfume, talcum powder and deodorant as they got into their wire-stiffened cotton swimsuits and tucked their hairdos under elastic caps, stiff white helmets embossed with sea-floral designs or softly shirred pastel wigs. It was the smell of women coming back from the pool, chlorinated water dripping from between their legs, from their fingertips. As they got into the showers there was the smell of hot water, soap, complete cleanliness dried by fresh rough towels—then more perfume, deodorant, hairspray, cosmetics, but never enough to completely eliminate the smell of chlorine and of wrinkled dampness.

It wasn't just the smell that fascinated Rhonda. It was also the sight of women. Eric, being younger, dressed with Helen and his sister if Bob didn't come along. Those were the times he and Rhonda liked to go crazy, running up and down the little streets of white curtains, tugging them back, twitching them, pretending to push each other inside, generally being bad, and sometimes, as a kind of reward, getting a glimpse of a huge, pink, wrinkled ass half-congealed into a girdle, or a pair of brown-nippled breasts falling out of a rigid ivory brassiere.

Eric eventually moved on permanently to the male world of jock straps and Brill Cream—the Men's Locker Room—while Rhonda remained, with her fantasies that grew both more circumspect and more daring. By the time she was eleven she no longer raced through the streets and alleys of the locker room, flicking aside curtains in the hope of surprising a woman's body. Instead, she practiced posing, shoulder strap casually falling off to reveal a small bud of breast, or towel draped artistically over her hipless form. She flung back her head, straddled the wooden bench and squirmed pleasantly. She stared at the two pubic hairs around her soft pink petals. And she waited.

Waited, not for some creepy kid to run up and down the corridors, but for a woman to make a mistake and come in.

Meanwhile, up in the lobby, Helen, so heavy now that

she never bothered to come downstairs, tapped her foot and eyed Rhonda penetratingly.

"It seems like it's taking you longer and longer to get dressed."

———————•———————

"Señor Columbus made his discovery in 1498 and also chloromycetin was discovered by a Venezuelan. We have thirty-two species of eagle and eighty percent of the goods made by Sears, Roebuck and Co. are made here. The River Orinoco is one thousand six hundred miles long and has a big mouth at the Atlantic Ocean. The highest uninterrupted waterfall in the world is here. It is Angel Falls and is named for Jimmy Angel, an American pilot who crashed in it. Caracas is our main city and it is three thousand one hundred and thirty-six feet high. Its average temperature is seventy degrees so it is very pleasant. . . ."

Dolores paused, discouraged less by her bad memory and worse syntax than by the complete irrelevance of what she was reciting. These English lessons, these facts to be memorized, all useless, watered down to be picturesque and nonthreatening. When she tried to do research on her own, into how much control the foreign oil companies exercised over the political situation, into why Bethlehem Steel and U.S. Steel had gotten such a foothold on the iron ore industry, she was told she was being provocative and ungenerous. Venezuela had the highest per capita income in South America and all this was due to American development. It was true that certain industrialists had sometimes misused their power . . . but times were changing. Betancourt was in power again.

It was curious. A month ago she'd been both ignorant and powerless, a nineteen-year-old ex-student and ex-mistress. Now she was suddenly viewed as the representative of the country. She'd met Betancourt, exchanged platitudes about her father. All her life she'd been taught to revere this president, as a man who'd spent twenty-one years either in exile or in prison in defense of his ideals. But now, he was in power and he was so frightened of the military on the Right, the Americans in the middle, and Fidel Castro on the Left, that he hardly dared take a step in any direction. He was a shrunken, tired-looking man who couldn't help letting his hand slip accidentally from her shoulder in friendly greeting to her full breast.

"The per capita income of Venezuela is the highest in South America. Besides oil and iron ore our principal income derives from the export of cacao and coffee. Along the coastal zone production is bananas, fish, and there are beach resorts. In the *llanos* or middle plains there are many goats and cat-tles. Coffee grows in the Andes as well as some wheat and potatoes. The government is in the process of di-ver-si-fying, what is called 'sowing the petroleum'; meaning we like to put our money into other things to make more money some day. . . ."

There was something very wrong with all this, but Dolores wasn't quite sure what to do about it, other than to follow, with greater than usual interest, the triumphs and problems of the new government in Havana.

————•————

Every year, at least since 1952 when Catalina Swimsuits had set up its own alternative to the Miss America Pageant, the far more exotic Miss Universe Contest had taken place in Long Beach, California. Rhonda's family was a great sup-porter of the pageant. Not only did they sit on the curb of Ocean Boulevard and watch the parade, but they followed the events on television as well, from the very first national anthem introductions through the swimsuit and evening gown competitions, right up to the final palpitating moments when the announcer opened the last envelope, the music surged expectantly and the newest Miss Universe burst into happy tears.

Nobody thought there was anything strange about this spectacle at the time. Rhonda's family certainly didn't. They used to compare the women fiercely at dinner and in front of the TV, both physically and geographically. Bob, a former information specialist in the Army and now the owner of a carpet store, liked to drop in bits of history and anthropology, perhaps to disguise his natural interest in the beauties' figures. Helen could be a little cruder; she sometimes made jokes about the sizes of their busts. Rhonda's own was hardly developing, a fact which seemed to please Helen, so obsessed these days with weight. "I never had this problem before I married," she would sigh, over the two huge mounds that covered her chest. "I was as flat as Rhonda."

When Rhonda looked at the foreign women she felt a glow and a wonder. What were they like, each one of them? What were the places like that they came from, that round, chin-tilted one from the Philippines, for instance, that tall lithe one from Iceland, that strapping freckled redhead from Australia.

Most years she got a chance to mingle with them in person, for there was always an overflow from the Lafayette Hotel into the Pacific Coast Club. Some years, damp and fresh, she'd run up from the Ladies' Locker Room and find the lobby full of mysterious women in suits and corsages, wearing wide ribbons: Miss Uruguay, Miss Canada, Miss India.

When she had been a child, they had sometimes stopped and smiled at her, stroked her head. At twelve Rhonda was awkward and yearning, with too much intensity.

Her mother found a picture of a naked woman in Rhonda's room. From now on, she said, Rhonda was too old for slumber parties.

If only she were beautiful—not Miss America, but something else, someone else. In school they offered Spanish or French as an elective. Rhonda signed up for both.

Dolores's roommate was from Sweden and could not have been more opposite, both in looks and in temperament; leggy, fair, careless and cheerful, Brigitte claimed she had starved her healthy body for weeks to win the contest, but that the money was worth it. She wanted to continue her medical studies in London and afterwards open up a clinic for women in Africa.

She introduced Dolores to Miss Portugal and Miss Sierra Leone, both of whom she'd met on the plane. Miss Portugal, a dimpled, satin-cheeked eighteen-year-old from Oporto, was the only one who was not anti-American or embarrassed at being in a beauty contest. Carmen ate her steak and salad at the welcoming lunch, wide-eyed and quiet, as the others discussed the de Beers diamond mines in Sierra Leone and Standard Oil in Venezuela. Brigitte mentioned that Long Beach, California, was an oil town too.

It was true. After lunch that first day the contestants were taken about the city on a tour bus. They saw the beaches and the amusement park, the harbor, the Douglas Aircraft plant and the new state college. They were even taken up to Signal Hill, an unincorporated outpost in the middle of the city that looked like a huge disheveled refuse heap. It had no wide boulevards fringed with palm trees or pink-and-green-stuccoed houses covered with bougainvillea, only row upon row of oil derricks and funny machines pumping up and down like rocking horses. The roads here were rough and dirty, the very air smelled of petroleum.

In spite of Dolores's late consuming interest in the oil industry, this was the first time she had seen a working oil field. She wanted to stop and walk around, to take pictures with her new camera. The chaperone, the former Miss California and now a stylish matron in a little blue hat and white gloves, masked her disapproval with trilling laughter.

"Well, just for a moment. . . ."

She watched helplessly as Dolores scampered about, photographing and thinking about industry's place in a socialist society.

———•———

Rhonda got up stiffly. The last float had gone by, the last white-gloved waving hand. She must be getting older; she felt a little silly this year as she made her way along through the crowds, evading Helen and her brother. Who in their right mind would wear long white gloves and high heels with a one-piece bathing suit? And you had to admit, the whole international thing was pretty hokey: having Miss Holland pose in wooden shoes, a white winged cap and a striped apron, while a tape recorder whined out a little dance.

All the same, it was still the one place where it was okay to stare. Ever since her mother had found that picture, Rhonda had been self-conscious. Her mother wouldn't even understand that they'd all been looking at it at the slumber party. It was Nancy's brother's, from his *Playboy* magazine. They'd spread it out on the floor in the middle of the night and practiced the same pose, draping bits of sheet over *that place*. It was a *joke,* Mom, Rhonda wanted to say. All the same it was Rhonda who'd taken the *Playboy* picture home with her, nobody could deny that; and maybe it was only Rhonda out of all the girls who had that funny feeling when she looked at the woman lying there smiling, smiling with her nice soft breasts, as if she were inviting Rhonda to touch them. Her mother had looked so funny when she found the photo: "*What* are you using this for?" she asked. Not even, Where did you get this?

And she'd snatched it from the drawer and torn it right in half, right through the breasts.

She didn't understand that Rhonda needed to know . . . what? Well, what they giggled about in gym class. That story about the woman who found the mouse in her closet, but it was really something to do with a hole in the wall and a man next door. She never understood that. And some girls talked about other girls who went all the way, like Jean who wore the thick lipstick and whose mother still let the older boy next door babysit because she didn't know what he and Jean were doing. But Rhonda didn't like boys very much. She just liked looking at women, even though she now knew that somehow it was bad.

She returned to the Pacific Coast Club, went downstairs to the Ladies' Locker Room. It was quiet today, for a Saturday. All the changing rooms stood open, their white curtains slack and sad in the thick, moist air.

————————•————————

Dolores was explaining the Cuban Revolution to Brigitte. It was the night after the swimsuit competition and they both needed to erase from their minds how it had felt to walk through the middle of a crowded auditorium, elevated on a runway like a turkey on a conveyor belt, wearing nothing but a white swimsuit, long white gloves and high heels.

"For some reason it's the gloves I hate most of all," said Brigitte. "Why cover up the hands, except to make us look like we can't resist, that we're clean goods as well?"

"Have you heard of a woman Celia Sánchez?" asked Dolores. "No? But she was up in the mountains, the Sierra Maestra, with Fidel Castro and the others. Knowing the way, leading and fighting. That is what I would like, *sabes?* I read their speeches now and the doctor's too, Che Guevara, and I am so happy, excited. For a people to be taking control. Soon they say they nationalize the industries, and give the land to the *gente* back from the *latifundistas*. And make everyone learn to read. What work there is to be done there, if one has the will to struggle. But struggle with others, not against them."

"When I become a doctor," said Brigitte, inspired, "I'll go there and work for them."

"Is it possible?" said Dolores. "To give up everything and start again? Better this time?"

————————•————————

Rhonda had escaped from her mother and Eric for a few moments, claiming that she had dropped her small purse on the beach and needed to retrieve it. It was the end of a boring day spent with the family, an entity she was coming more and more to despise. If it wasn't her brother kicking and pinching her, it was her mother remarking on everything with that sour smirk of unhappiness and condemnation. Why was she so unhappy, why so suspicious that everyone was cheating them or lying? And why did her father ignore her or believe what Helen said about her? Helen had probably told him about the *Playboy* picture. . . .

Rhonda walked along the edge of the water. It was getting on late afternoon; the sky had that white, blowsy feeling it got sometimes before sunset, when the ocean turned skittish and cold, the sand flared up under your feet. Seagulls cried hopelessly, callously.

She was thinking about the woman whose breasts her mother had torn in half. She couldn't help it, she still thought about them. And that funny feeling kept coming into her *place*; lately she had taken to rubbing it, not just on a bench or with a towel, but with her hand. She would die if anyone ever saw her, she knew that no one else ever did it, but more and more she wanted to. It felt so good, it felt like something built up, she didn't know what, because nothing ever happened. She would do it for a while, until she almost started to feel uncomfortable or in pain from the tingling and the want. And then she would stop, feeling unsatisfied and strange but also excited.

And now she was doing it again in her mind, thinking of the breasts and wondering how whatever happened, happened. But what? But what? And suddenly Rhonda was overcome by the immense weariness of being a child. It wasn't fair never to understand, and to be pushed around and made to feel bad about everything.

She was approaching one of the lifeguard stations. Having completely forgotten, though perhaps intentionally, about Helen and Eric waiting in the lobby of the Pacific Coast Club, Rhonda decided it would be fun to climb the wooden ladder to the platform and to sit for a while. And think.

Dolores had escaped from the pageant temporarily, from her chaperone and the various officials. She was definitely not interested in the planned trip to Disneyland and so, during the flurry of boarding the bus, she had slipped away, back to her room to grab a scarf, dark glasses and coat. Thus disguised she'd come down to the beach to walk and to wonder what would happen if she suddenly flew straight from Los Angeles to Havana. Miss Venezuela was a full-time job; they had appearances scheduled for her all year in Caracas and around the country. A life waited for her there, though it was not, if it had ever been, her life.

She had climbed onto the platform of the lifeguard station and was sitting against the wind with her back to the warm, weatherworn door, when she saw the head of a young girl pop up over the side. The girl's eyes widened so comically that Dolores had to laugh.

"Don't be afraid, *chiquita*," she said. "I won't eat you."

The girl hesitated, then bashfully continued her climb. She was a gangly, awkward thing with big brown eyes and cowlicky hair. Her arms were rather muscular; she had a scrape on her knee, and elbow as well. She was wearing a skirt and sandals and carrying a white cardigan sweater. She seated herself at the far end of the platform and asked, "Are you in the contest?"

Dolores shrugged with some embarrassment, then decided to be sophisticated. "Miss Venezuela, Dolores María Angelus Otero, at your service."

"Gee," said the girl slowly, staring hard and turning away, beet red. "Gee," she repeated.

"Please," said Dolores, a little impatiently, but also kindly, "What is your name?"

"Oh. Rhonda. Rhonda Metcalfe. Wow," she said. "You're really from Venezuela?" And she seemed suddenly to have recovered the use of her tongue. "What's Venezuela like? I don't know anything about it. I mean, I know about Mexico, we went to Tijuana once anyway. I'm taking Spanish, you know. I mean, how could you know, but I am. *Cómo estás?* See, that's because I want to travel and do everything when

I'm older. I can hardly wait, I can't stand being twelve, I mean, sometimes I don't feel like I'm twelve. I don't know, I feel so old sometimes but they treat me like a baby all the time. I wish I was as old as *you*. I wish I could be like you, it must be so *neat* to wear all those dresses and maybe get to be Miss Universe and meet everybody from other countries. . . ." Rhonda broke off. Dolores was staring at her in bewilderment. "Do I talk too fast?" she exclaimed solicitously.

Dolores burst out laughing and removed her dark glasses. To Rhonda she looked less like Nefertiti than Sophia Loren, redolent of sex and mystery and luxury. Dolores said, "It is just that, I am not so much used to, you are talking about very many things all at once. But you are a nice girl," she added.

Rhonda sighed and dropped her eyes for a moment, breathing hard. Her mind was busy with impossible schemes: asking Miss Venezuela to dinner, seeing if she could stay with them during her visit; dropping in on her someday in Venezuela. She was so excited that she could hardly think straight. "Do you have a little sister?" she burst out.

"I have no one," Dolores said, and her gaze swept the sea tragically. "I am now planning to be a revolutionary."

"Can I be your little sister?" Rhonda asked and then was aware of how ridiculous this sounded. She blushed again, up to the roots of her cowlick.

Yet for the first time Dolores really seemed to look at her and a soft yet spirited expression came into her large painted eyes. "I will be your sister, little one," she said, as if making a promise. "In my heart I will think of you. That we will both have better lives from this day forward."

It was so wonderful, her saying that, that Rhonda could hardly believe Miss Venezuela was talking to her. Perhaps Dolores was just being friendly, perhaps she was making some deeper vow to herself alone. At any rate Dolores suddenly reached over and took Rhonda's hand and squeezed it.

"Just be careful, my young friend, with the boys. Watch out," Dolores said, eyes narrowed.

It was on the tip of Rhonda's tongue to exclaim that she didn't even like boys anyway, but she didn't want to spoil the moment. She yearned into Dolores's lovely face, murmuring, "Okay."

This was the scene, then, that met Helen's eyes as she approached the lifeguard station in the course of looking for Rhonda all over the beach and fearing the worst: her twelve-year-old daughter holding hands with some dark, foreign-looking woman in a raincoat and scarf.

"My lands!" she gasped, standing stock-still in the windy sand.

"Who's that lady with Rhonda?" Eric said, and his piercing young voice carried over to the lifeguard station so that Rhonda turned around with a jerk of horror.

"My mother," she muttered to Dolores.

"Rhonda, you come right down off of that platform. Right now."

"Good-bye," said Rhonda, tortured, to Dolores, with one last look.

Dolores put her sunglasses back on and looked mysterious. "Good-bye, Rona," she said, squeezing the girl's hand. *"Que tengas una vida muy feliz."* She ignored Helen and the yapping Eric at her heels.

"Who is that woman?" Helen hissed when Rhonda crossed slowly over the sand to them. "Just who is that women you were holding hands with, Rhonda Metcalfe?"

"Miss Venezuela," sighed Rhonda. *"Just* Miss Venezuela, that's all."

And for once her mother had nothing to say.

———— • ————

For years afterward, long after she could quite remember Dolores's liquid gaze and firm grasp, Rhonda cultivated a special fascination for the country of Venezuela. She dressed up as a cowgirl from the *llanos* for a skit on different countries once; she wrote a paper or two on Venezuela in school.

She continued taking Spanish all the way through college. And naturally she nursed a secret preference for dark-eyed women who looked like Sophia Loren, though she ended up with a perfectly nice woman from Kansas, a freckle-face named Mary Sue.

When Rhonda went into the Peace Corps she was stationed in Bolivia. She managed to visit Venezuela several times, to sit on a bit of beach overlooking the sea, to smell the strong, familiar tang of salt and oily water, to feel a little silly but somehow at home.

Of course she never ran into the former Miss Venezuela. Dolores had jumped bail as the country's queen long ago and had moved to Cuba. She became a lawyer, married, and adopted three children, one of whom she named Rona. It might have been coincidence. It might have been how she kept her promise.

Walking on the Moon

One

It seemed so different at first. Almost as if I'd never been here before. The train station, for instance—they were renovating the Düsseldorf Hauptbahnhof. Instead of stepping off the train from Hamburg and following the crowd to the spacious lobby with its numerous shops and newsstands, the way I remembered, I was shunted with the other passengers along rickety overhead corridors and stairways directly to the exit. I found myself unexpectedly outside the massive construction work, staring at the city without the slightest sense of recognition.

But then, it had been twelve years.

————•————

All my life I've loved rainy weather. As a child I was always happiest—broodingly happiest—on those infrequent days in Southern California when winter storms flooded the streets and everyone else stayed inside. I recall carrying my family's one umbrella down swollen pathways in the park, standing under dripping trees, reciting Edgar Allan Poe. Later, as an adolescent romantic, I discovered Rilke: *"Whoever you are, go out into the evening/ leaving your room, of which you know each bit;/ your house is the last before the infinite."*

It was raining when I arrived in Düsseldorf and it rained steadily throughout the spring I spent there. The German grandparents of a high school friend had found me a job in an Evangelical Girls' Home, a Mädchensheim. I was to work a half a day cleaning in exchange for room and board and a hundred marks a month. I arrived with my suitcases packed with books and spent my traveling allowance the first week on the collected works of Goethe, Rilke, Mann and Hesse. I hardly spoke any German but expected to progress very rapidly on my own. I was eighteen and had graduated early.

The twenty or so other girls in the Mädchensheim were almost all dental hygiene students and most were, like me, away from home for the first time. They wore white stretch knee socks and mini-skirts and giggled a lot. In the beginning they invited me to their rooms, showed me photographs of their families and their vacations in Yugoslavia and invariably asked me why I had come to Germany. I had no photographs, wore embroidered jeans and no bra, and said I wanted to be a writer. After two weeks they left me alone.

It didn't really bother me then. I was much happier outside the Mädchensheim, exploring the city with its churches, bookstores and museums. I bought an umbrella and caught a perpetual cold in the damp Hofgarten, sitting on soaked benches, feeling a delicious sadness in the knowledge that I was far from home, was friendless and would probably die of pneumonia.

Of course I, like all the others, had a roommate. Her name was Edeltrude and she was also a dental hygiene student. She had bleached canary yellow hair, a rough crop of acne and an insatiable appetite for women's magazines and chocolate. Our narrow room was divided straight down the middle; her walls were covered with cut-out pages of fashionable models, her shelves held dozens of stuffed animals and dolls in Bavarian costume. I had only books and scraps of paper full of poetry and case endings.

Edeltrude and I never talked much. Every day after her morning classes she'd return to fling herself on her bed with a new assortment of magazines and a few candy bars, and there she'd lie for the rest of the afternoon, turning pages, melting chocolate on her thick pale tongue and picking at her face. I read or wrote at the table by the window, painstakingly looking up every third word in *Siddhartha* and staring at the rain that beat against the glass.

More often than not I went out.

I liked to stand on the banks of the Rhine, quoting Rilke softly: *"As one who has sailed across an unknown sea/ among this rooted folk I am alone"*; or wander through the narrow, cobbled streets of the Altstadt. I dreamily watched the swans in the canal or hunted up picturesque cafes where I could sit for hours undisturbed, writing in my journal (*"We are all strangers in this universe"*) or jotting down poems (*"We are all strangers in this universe. . . ."*).

If I was at all disappointed in Düsseldorf it was because it was not the pastoral Germany of my real and mental picture books. After being half-leveled by Allied bombs during the war, it had been built back up into a modern city with wide boulevards and fashionable arcades. Tourist literature referred to it as the "Paris of the North," but I would have preferred a village in the Black Forest. I usually tried to avoid the city center in favor of the romantic park, but occasionally found myself hurrying past one of the expensive show windows on the Königsallee with their often futuristic displays. It was 1969, the year of NASA and the astronauts' Apollo flight. One department store, I remember, had a window lined with foil, with silver-skinned mannequins dressed in hot pants and helmets flying gravityless through the air.

My job at the Mädchensheim was simple. After breakfast I was supposed to put the chairs on the tables and sweep and wash the floor of the dining room. I then scrubbed the upstairs hall and watered the plants. Before lunch I usually helped cut up potatoes or slice vegetables in the kitchen. Finally I set the tables and carried dishes out to them for the noontime meal.

That was all, but I hated it. I managed to get away to my

room each morning for an hour or two, to pursue my grammar and to get out from under the eye of the housekeeper, Frau Kosak. I called her the Cossack to myself. She was a refugee from East Germany and she had heavy, stumpy legs wrapped entirely in flesh-colored, elastic bandages. Over these she wore hose with a black seam up the back. Frau Kosak was a hard worker and disapproved of me. She had a tread like an industrial robot, however, so I could usually get out of my room in time to be busy in a corner.

The names of the two women in the kitchen I don't remember. I don't even remember what they looked like. But they had a half-witted helper who still sticks in my mind. Called Anneliese, she was six feet tall, with tangled black hair and two raisin-purple eyes, intently insane. Her speech was garbled and rough. From the moment she saw me she took a liking to me and often tried to touch my face. I usually met her in the cellar where she worked scrubbing potatoes or washing linen. It terrified me when she loomed up out of a dark doorway; I believed her capable of anything.

Upstairs all was harmony and *Gemütlichkeit*. The manager of the Mädchensheim was a full-bodied, placid woman by the name of Frau Holtz. She tried to take a motherly interest in me, was always suggesting I go out with the other girls or take German lessons. When I resisted her efforts, with mingled arrogance and embarrassment, she began to look sorry for me. I used to go down to see if there were any letters only when I knew she was out of the office.

Usually there were no letters. My mother wrote once a week; my friends were more erratic. They were still in high school, getting ready for college by smoking a lot of dope. What did they care about my melancholic ecstasies over rain and Rilke? They might have been interested if I'd been meeting German hippies, but they were definitely not excited about an Evangelical Girls' Home filled with dental hygiene students, or a life that was lived—more and more half-heartedly—through word-by-word translations from the dictionary.

My self-induced sadness began to feel more like loneliness, my angst like mere homesickness and my explorations like the pacing of a prisoner.

I decided I needed a friend and I looked around to find one.

———————•———————

I came to Düsseldorf today from Hamburg, where I'd been staying with two friends, Nathalie and Clara. I don't know them well, and before this trip I hardly knew them at all.

I met them last summer in Canada. I was sitting on a bench in Vancouver's Stanley Park, watching the sunset and thinking on and off about my life in Seattle. I wasn't on vacation, just taking a day or two off from work and friends. Nathalie and Clara were down by the water's edge, throwing in stones and sticks, and chasing each other, laughing. It was pleasant to see them against the rose and yellow of the sky, the one woman so light and snub, with electric blonde hair, the other olive-skinned and brunette, with an oval face and sloping shoulders.

I watched them for half an hour and returned their smiles. I was glad when I saw them coming towards me, then taken aback. The accent of their greeting was strong and obvious.

They were German.

Neither Nathalie nor Clara could tell I was an American. They hadn't learned to distinguish a mild West Coast intonation from a Canadian accent. I found it ironic when their faces changed; no, they weren't too fond of Americans. Two months they'd spent traveling across Canada. They were due to fly out of Vancouver's airport the next day and it had never occurred to them, apparently, to take a side trip south of the border.

"But you seem different," they told me carefully.

And Nathalie, snub-nosed and elfin, assured me, "We like you."

We spent the evening together and before we parted we agreed that when I came to Europe this year I would visit them in Hamburg. For some reason I never told them that I had lived in Germany once, a long time ago, had lived and worked in Düsseldorf for six months, in an Evangelical Girls' Home.

————•————

There had always been a girl at the Mädchensheim who interested me. Although I never talked to her—I never talked to any of them by now—I often watched her. She was a little older than the rest, with an awkwardness that made her shy away from furniture and objects as if they were obstacles to her uncertain progress through the world. I had heard her called "the Duck" and, sad to say, it fit. She took small, almost mincing steps that made her look like she was waddling. This effect was emphasized by the breadth of her behind and her narrow, forward-thrusting shoulders. She was always out of alignment, always looked as if she were carrying a burden.

Her face was mannish, at least I thought so at the time and with repugnance. It was square and heavy at jaw and forehead. The skin was downy brown; she wore her hair clipped like a boy's, with a straight part on the left. When she laughed she shook all over and put her hand to her mouth. She never made a sound.

I had noticed from the first or second day that she had no friends. She would stand apart as we all waited outside the dining room for the dinner or lunch bell to ring. At meals she gobbled her food and left early. She was the only girl in the Mädchensheim to have a room by herself.

Her name was Käthe.

It was about a month after my arrival at the Mädchensheim that we first spoke to each other. It was a wet April evening and I was returning after hours spent wandering in the Hofgarten. I was soaked beneath my umbrella, having let it down romantically, but unwisely, to feel the rain on my face. I was melancholy and hungry, since I'd missed lunch and probably dinner; my only hope was that Edeltrude might give me some of her chocolate. As I walked along the street I saw the Duck, hunching and waddling her way towards me. She, too, carried an umbrella; she, too, looked damp underneath it. Her short hair was slicked back on her head like seal's fur. She protected a book in one hand.

At first I thought I'd cross the street to avoid her; she must have had a similar idea, for she paused, jerked spasmodically, turned, then turned back again and came straight on. I couldn't run away after that performance; it was too clearly an unconscious imitation of my own. I came straight on as well. We met at the Mädchensheim's outer door.

"*Guten Abend,*" she said in a low voice.

"*Guten Abend.*"

I saw her break into a smile and wondered for an alarmed minute if she were going to start her silent, hysteric laugh. Then I noticed that she was staring at the book I held in my hand. It was the same as hers: a bright yellow paperback copy of *Also Sprach Zarathustra.* Hers was just more dogeared than mine.

"So," she said. "You are reading Nietzsche?"

"Yes." We were both surprised. The American girl, the dental hygiene student—both reading Nietzsche?

"But can you understand it?" she asked.

"Well, some. I read it in English first. That helps."

I had not been reading it at all that day, or any day. It was filled with too many hard words. I only liked to carry it around because it made me feel scholarly and important.

"Nietzsche is our greatest poet," she said humbly.

I thought I was misunderstanding. "He's not a poet, is he? He's a philosopher."

Käthe looked amazed at my ignorance. Opening her copy to a heavily underscored and scribbled page, she read aloud:

"*You must discover a love which will bear not only punishment but all guilt as well! You must discover a justice which will acquit everyone excepting the judge!*"

"That," she concluded rapturously, "that is poetry. What a soul that man had. He understood so much."

Now it was my turn to be humble. "You've read him very thoroughly." I didn't want to admit I'd hardly comprehended a word of it. It was her margin notes that had impressed me.

Abruptly the suppressed, mouth-covering laugh shook her. I noticed that her eyes were bluegray, very large and clear. They seemed to be unconscious of the gyrations of her lower face; they looked sad and far-away.

"Have you missed dinner too?" I asked nervously.

She nodded, still twitching, but as if the fit had passed.

"Do you have any food?" My question popped out unexpectedly. Was I that desperate for company? Especially when I could see that she was more than a little strange?

"Come," she said and started through the door. "I will feed you."

We went inside and up the stairs and I was grateful not to meet anyone. Her room seemed larger than mine, but that was because it had only one bed. Everything was very neat. The top sheet of the bed was folded back severely, a pair of pajamas lay across it like a rigid human form. There was a small library standing straight and dignified on the table by the window: novels, poetry, more Nietzsche and one volume of astronomy.

Once inside her room Käthe grew calm and hostess-like. She went right to a large cupboard and revealed a miniature grocery store and kitchen. Crackers, cookies, sausage, cheese, even a half liter of milk. And a hotplate that, she informed me serenely, was illegal. I was surprised but pleased at the change in her. She wasn't so odd, after all, if she could put on some water for soup and start carving sausage and cheese. She even seemed to have discovered a maternal tone.

"Sit down, please. Let me get you some milk. I didn't see you at lunch. Did you miss that too?"

"I get tired of that dining room," I admitted. "Everyone talking about stupid things."

"And I too," she said. "I often eat here. I like it better."

We smiled at each other for the first time. I was relieved to see that when Käthe smiled she looked completely ordinary, even warm. Not a trace of hysteria.

I drank the milk carefully, obediently. It had a tepid, sweet taste that I found comforting. I liked being here, I decided all at once. And it was definitely better than begging a candy bar from Edeltrude and watching her cut her toenails.

I turned to Käthe's books, pulled the astronomy volume out of its strict alignment. Big and beautiful, though a little worn, it had full color plates of galaxies and solar systems. It made me remember an astronomy book I once had and a game I used to play with it. When I was sad as a child or trying hard to settle on who I was and what I loved, I'd open my book to the diagram of the planets and position myself out among them, a satellite, an angel, a flying speck of feeling. Only when I had safely left Earth behind could I let myself return, sometimes slowly, falling with faint gravity, sometimes leaping over meteors and asteroids, round Saturn's rings and Jupiter's moons, past the hot red sands of Mars, the cold windy craters of the moon, our moon, so different up close, so forbidding. At that point the earth would seem very welcome, now familiar, its continents revolving from brown to green to white, its oceans swimming dark blue to light. From space I would chose again my country, my city, my friends and family, those I remembered, those I loved, those that told me, *home is here.*

"Are you interested in astronomy?" I asked quickly, to stop myself thinking of how far away home really was.

Käthe turned back to the cupboard, busied herself arranging crackers on a plate. "It's my brother's," she said, as if I were trespassing. I put the book back.

Abruptly she said, "You are lonely. Am I right?"

I hadn't yet admitted that, to myself or anyone. "It's not so easy, always, being here. I guess I miss my. . . . But I'm learning a lot. Everything is very new and interesting."

The Duck gave me a penetrating bluegray look as she set the plate down in front of me. "Eat, eat," she urged, and then, with hardly a change of tone, "All people are lonely."

"Oh, I don't know." I filled my mouth so full I could barely articulate. "I'm not lonely right now."

"All people are lonely," Käthe insisted. "It is their fate."

I nodded politely and stole a glance at the copy of *Zarathustra*.

"Are *you* lonely?" I ventured.

Käthe stirred a packet of soup into the boiling water. Her shoulders began to heave and for an awful moment I thought she was sobbing. But it was only her laugh, silent, compressed, epileptic. I thought of telling her that to laugh like that was probably unhealthy. My grandmother used to tell me that about suppressed hiccoughs. "Let them out, Elizabeth," she would say. "Or else you'll get an irregular heartbeat."

"Do you really want to be a dental hygienist?" I blurted.

"Ha." Käthe stopped laughing and sneered.

"I suppose it pays well."

"Ha."

"It seems funny to think of you, I mean, you don't seem like the kind of person who, I mean, like Edeltrude. . . ."

Käthe stirred the soup violently. "Do you think I want to be studying the insides of mouths? Do you really think I am like the rest of them?"

"No."

"And yet, what should I do?" She began a waddling march around the small room, stopping to look at me after each sentence. "I am twenty-three. My parents took me out of school when I was fourteen. They put me in a shop to work. It was so my brother could go to the University. To study physics. They said I wasn't smart enough to go to the University. That I was a girl. It was not necessary." Käthe suddenly stared at me suspiciously. "You have been to the University?"

"Next fall." I wanted to explain that in America it wasn't such a big deal. Lots of people went. Lots dropped out too. I had already been thinking of dropping out.

But Käthe interrupted me. "All this," she said, waving to

her Nietzsche books, "I have done on my own. Studied on my own."

"But," I fumbled for the words, "couldn't you have gone to the University when you got older?"

She glared at me quickly, then her eyes turned clear and far-away again. They were really wonderful eyes.

"It's too complicated," she said. "Other things happened."

———————•———————

Nathalie is a secretary, takes dance and judo classes in the evening, organizes against NATO and nuclear power, studies Italian and sews her own clothes. She's come out since we met in Vancouver, a process that was detailed in the long, intensely written letters she sent me over the past year. She fell in love with a woman in one of her political groups.

Clara, who only mailed a postcard or added a P.S. from time to time, works as a gardener for the city of Hamburg. She's been married and divorced and is, like me, now unattached. Unlike me she's never loved a woman, but she wonders if she might, someday. She is in therapy and sometimes sings and shouts to loud rock music in her room, swaying back and forth with anger. Otherwise she is a quiet and modest woman who likes plants and art books.

They don't seem so different from the women who are my friends in America. And, in fact, Americans and Germans have much in common: not only are we held in contempt by the rest of the world, but we despise each other's nationality as well. I can't be in Germany without sometimes thinking of the Jews and their destruction. They can't hear my American accent without remembering Vietnam or being reminded of the military bases full of soldiers and nuclear missiles that overrun their country now.

And yet—we're women. We're feminists. They tell me stories of smashing porn shop windows in Hamburg's red light district. I talk about spraypainting sexist billboards. We share feminist magazines and books, complain about all the meetings we go to, discuss abortion rights, gay rights, racism, the growing problem of violence against women, rape and battering. We talk and talk and have everything to say.

The only thing we don't share is language. They talk to me in English. I answer in English. Yet when they talk to each other in German I sometimes understand them. I don't want them to talk in German; it reminds me of things I'd forgotten.

"And so, you know, our group was . . . it was like our whole political group was in a. . . ." Nathalie turned to Clara in frustration. *"Was ist Niedergeschlagenheit auf Englisch?"*

"Depression," I said automatically.

They both stared at me.

I had to explain. "Well, I studied a little German once, a long time ago. There are a few words I remember. . . ."

Clara and Nathalie laughed, surprised. "You never told us! Now we have to be careful how we talk about you!"

I laughed too, repeated, "I only remember a few words. . . ."

Yes, some words, very well.

----•----

I used to meet Kathe outside the dental hygiene school and we would walk for hours. In the evenings we retired to her room to eat cheese and crackers and discuss philosophy. All through April and far into May we sat at the table staring out at the rain while Käthe helped me with my German by setting me translations of Nietzsche.

I remember we discussed, among other things, the concept of *Heimweh.* Homesickness. I said I missed particular things sometimes—the beaches back home, a favorite picture on the wall, a tune my mother used to play on the piano. Käthe accused me of being literal-minded. *Heimweh,* for her, was a universal condition. She said she didn't miss people or

objects she'd left behind; rather her yearning was for some
state of mind she obscurely believed was possible.

"What state of mind?"

"Freedom."

Because German is a language that capitalizes all nouns, I
even heard them that way: *Freiheit, Angst, Heimweh.* All were
strange and meaningful and out of reach. Käthe's conversation sometimes sounded to me like a poem of Rilke's, lonely,
aching, suggesting the saddest possibilities. I didn't argue
with her that she was already free, but instead read aloud to
her my favorite Rilke poem, ending:

> *"To you is left (unspeakably confused)*
> *your life, gigantic, ripening, full of fears,*
> *so that it, now hemmed in, now grasping all,*
> *is changed in you by turn to stone and stars."*

"Exactly," Käthe said. "Full of fears."

Of course, most of the time she drove me crazy. I hated to
see her furtive shakes of laughter. I hated the way she wad-
dled, the way she hovered uncertainly, toe to heel to toe, on
the edge of a curb, waiting for the light to change.

"It's no good," I tried to tell her. "The light will change
when it's ready. You'll only get yourself run over."

She rushed me through sites I'd already visited—the museums, the churches, the Altstadt, pointing out a history she
barely understood herself with a dictatorial and frantic air.
She demanded the right to buy me useless little souvenirs,
insisted on feeding me at every possible opportunity. She
dragged me into cafes to fill my plate with strudels *mit Schlag*
and *Apfelkuchen.* She would grow moody, sighing and urging
me to eat, then suddenly, a fit of animation would strike her.
She would ask, "What does the *Übermensch* mean to you?"

Flippant, irritated, I answered, "The astronauts."

"*Genau,*" she said seriously. "What an act of will to think
of reaching the moon."

"Oh, come on," I muttered in English.

But Käthe would not be dissuaded. "I love to think of
them, alone in space. How brave they must be."

I was glad that none of my real friends at home would ever meet her, especially when she talked like this. At other times I almost clung to her, feeling she was the only one who understood me now.

I knew, for instance, that Käthe and only Käthe could appreciate the beauty and significance of the four statues outside the Kunsthalle. The four women stood in two couples; one pair held hands, the other had their arms around each other's shoulders. They were all of marble, Grecian in form and face, with flowing robes. One carried an artist's palette, another a book, one a temple and another a lyre. They were Muses of course, but I saw them as creators, strong, forward-looking, loving each other and their work.

"I would like them to be my gravestone," said Käthe the first time I brought her to see them.

I felt the same. I said, "Oh, don't be ridiculous."

Two

I said to myself, It's cheating to get a map, but I got one anyway. I didn't look at it, stuffed it in my pocket. A part of me insisted, You'll never forget. Another part wavered, It was so long ago, so many things have happened in the meantime.

I kept standing in front of the boarded up Düsseldorf Hauptbahnhof. It was warm for early April, sunny and dry. Midday. Finally I tied my sweater around my waist and started off. I was going to the Mädchensheim but I had no idea what I was looking for.

It wasn't so far from the station. I had walked to the Hauptbahnhof often enough, to mail letters, to buy American books and magazines, to take the train to Cologne to see the cathedral. Now I was only walking the way back to the Mädchensheim. I didn't really recognize any of the stores, or the street names or even the city's general configuration. Still, I didn't have to look at the map. The sidewalk began to speak to me. The sidewalk, hot under the spring sun, said, "You were so unhappy here." The sidewalk remembered my homesickness; a sad taskmaster, it instructed me where to cross the street, where to turn. My heart beat rapidly, painfully, and my breath stuck in my throat. I didn't know the way but my feet remembered it all. This way. Now this.

It was no more than ten minutes away, on a street I suddenly recalled as having been bombed-out and never rebuilt on one side. Now there was a parking lot there. On the other side of the street was a row of thick houses and walls with heavy doors. I couldn't remember the number but I recognized the door. Right in the middle of the row; it said, Open me. I walked into a corridor, a courtyard. There was the Mädchensheim, with a garden. It all seemed so much smaller. I looked up and saw an open window on the second floor. I told myself, "That was Käthe's room."

———————•———————

Near the end of May there was a holiday, a long weekend, when Käthe asked me to come home with her to meet her family. She said her brother was coming.

"I thought you didn't like him?"

We were sitting in her room on a mild spring evening, in front of the open window. Below us, in the garden, the dental hygiene students crossed and recrossed, laughing, arms linked. Their white knee socks shone like birch trees in the twilight—sturdy, but somehow transparent. That evening it made me sad to see the girls, with their pleasure in each other's company. They were Käthe's and my age, but they seemed so much younger. They were all younger than I had ever been. I wouldn't have been caught dead at home with my arm around a friend.

"I never said that," Käthe protested.

I shrugged and lit another Attika. I'd taken up smoking in the last few weeks, to make myself more interesting. "Not that I blame you," I exhaled. "Didn't you once tell me that he was the reason you couldn't finish school?"

"Don't ask me such questions. It was not his fault. Anyway, I've forgiven him."

Käthe leaned out the window so I couldn't see her face. After a minute she said dreamily, "I want to fly. Down in the garden among them. Shall I try?"

Her broad behind stuck out ludicrously, rectangular as a box of laundry soap turned sideways. Go ahead, jump, I thought, yet I almost put my arms around her waist to stop her falling.

"You never talk about your childhood," I said, jostling her at the window, letting my ashes drift down into the blossoming cherry tree beneath us. In the garden Edeltrude was walking with another girl. She looked up at me and Käthe, waved, then whispered something to her friend. I waved too, casually, and took a step backwards.

"But if I take you there to see it?" Käthe still stood looking out. She seemed oddly insistent.

"Come back inside, they're talking about us," I said. "Yes, I'll go." I added in a slightly bitter voice that it might be a welcome change from the Evangelical Girls' Home.

It was late when we arrived at the small town north of Dortmund; nevertheless Käthe's mother insisted that we eat something. She didn't embrace her daughter or make any sign of affection other than a worried twisting of her broad forehead. "So you're all right, then?" it could have meant. Or, "The same as usual, I see."

Käthe's mother was a big woman, not so much fat as lumpy, as if she had pebbles under her skin and rocks tucked into her faded cotton dress. The twisting of her forehead was habitual with her; it marred what otherwise might have been a handsome face. For it was broad and strongly molded, the eyes the same shade as Käthe's, a light bluegray, the color of a lonely pond in autumn.

Frau König led us right to the kitchen, roomy and bright, almost painfully clean. Out of the small refrigerator came milk and orange juice. From the pantry she brought liverwurst, Jarlsberg and fresh butter. Thick slices of bread she cut for us, holding the firm loaf to her chest.

Käthe gobbled stolidly as she always did, intent on her food, silent. Her mother plied me with coffee and with slow, distinct questions, as if I were deaf, a lip-reader: "How do you like Germany?" "What do you do here?" "How many in your family?"

Her forehead twisted as if a pellet of pain were planted between skin and skull. From time to time Frau König put a hand up to smooth the wrinkling, but her voice continued steady: Was I studying? What did my father do? Was I staying long in Germany?

I began to feel that the questions, in spite of being directed at me, were a means of circumscribing her daughter. Like nets they drew closer and closer, like warnings they took on an ominous tone: How had I met Käthe? Did we spend much time together? When was I leaving Düsseldorf?

Stumbling over even familiar German words, I found myself lying in the effort to staunch Frau König's curiosity. I gave more information about my family, not to mention my impressions, my plans, my memories, than I ever had to Käthe . . . and I gave them entirely new meanings. Oh, I was just a student who'd finished high school early, over here to get to know the language better. My father taught data processing at a technical school, my mother was a housewife who enjoyed the piano. I had two younger brothers, both football players. We lived in a three-bedroom house with a two-car garage, though we only had one. . . . I really liked Germany very much, though of course I would be glad to see my family again. I hoped at the end of the summer to do a little traveling before I went home. I'd love to see Munich and Salzburg and Zurich. I had heard so much about them.

I naturally said nothing about wanting to be a writer or about having run off to Germany to immerse myself in poetry and melancholy. Instead I talked of Düsseldorf—such a cultural city—and of the Mädchensheim—so many nice girls. I didn't look at Käthe as I talked for fear of seeing my betrayal in her large eyes. But what had she expected? That I would tell her mother stories of evenings spent discussing Nietzsche? You didn't talk to anyone's mother about your real feelings and thoughts. You tried to seem disgustingly normal, in the hope she wouldn't probe deeper. It seemed very important, as Frau König stared at me with her forehead twisting and as Käthe spread yet another slice of bread with butter, that I appear as unthreatening, as cheerful, as innocent as possible.

"So," Frau König said finally, satisfied or perhaps just tired of my ingenuity. "My Käthe has found a friend."

"Ja, ja." I nodded my head up and down vigorously. "She's teaching me German."

Käthe ate silently on.

————•————

Clara was talking about her group therapy. How she fell in love with a sensitive man after he came into the circle and described how he could never follow up on his attraction to a woman. He would feel initially infatuated, but after a few meetings, a few nights, suddenly he couldn't stand her.

"So what happened between you?" I asked.

"After a few nights he couldn't stand me."

We were sitting in her room with a pot of tea between us. Clara was wearing a light Indian shirt and her dark hair was pulled into a short ponytail. She smiled at me.

"And then he *talked* about it, about us, in front of the group. Was I embarrassed." Growing serious she said, "They asked me to talk about my side of it and all of a sudden I was going on and on about how much I hated my father, how he never treated me with respect, how in fact he *disrespected* me."

Nathalie whirled in. "Oh, tea, good. What a day I've had. I finally told that boss to leave me alone. I suppose I'm out of work soon."

Clara and I had to laugh at this juxtaposition. "Have you ever had therapy, Nathalie?" I asked.

"Of course, of course. *Natürlich*," she said, pouring herself tea and opening a parcel filled with cream cakes. "When I first became aware of my attraction to Agatha, that's exactly where I went. To the psychiatrist." She paused to stuff her mouth with cake. "Delicious, my favorite kind! So of course he tells me I hate my father. I tell him, sorry, no, it's my mother I don't get along with. My father went off a long time ago."

Clara interrupted, "He tells her she hates her father for abandoning her. While my therapist and group say, 'Oh, you don't really hate your father. You're just mad at Heinrich. He's the one who has problems, you should have tried harder to make him get over his dislike for you!'"

We all started laughing then, mouths full of crumbs and cream.

"Have you ever had therapy?" they asked me.

I shook my head. "No, I hated myself and my parents about equally. It all balanced out in the end. I like them now. My mother went back to school and got a degree in music. My dad retired and goes fishing. They're divorced of course."

————— • —————

The visit to Käthe's home was marked by many meals, each more awkward than the last. Käthe's father turned up at lunch the next day. He was unremarkable, except for his gnarled hands, out of character in one who worked in an office. They were bent and discolored, like lumps of glass unblown and melting. I was fascinated in a horrible way, staring at them clench their way towards dishes and bowls, wounded animals groping over the white tablecloth.

We ate sauerbraten and carrots and potatoes with thick gravy, and cucumber salad with sour cream and apple torte with whipped cream, course after course, ending with chocolate and coffee. I had never eaten so much or been so polite in my life. I praised each dish Frau König brought to the table and followed her constant injunctions to eat, to eat, with enthusiasm. I wanted to please her, I wanted her to like me, if only to make up for Käthe's firm silence.

After lunch Frau König took us shopping while her husband napped. In the car I sat in the front seat while Käthe huddled monosyllabically in the back. Frau König drove with surprising speed and expertness and pointed out the few sites of interest: a fifteenth-century church, an auto parts factory, a heavy wooden cross on one of the hills to mark the site of a munitions plant that operated during the war; the same plant, Frau König told me simply, where Herr König's hands had been burned.

It was a small and perfectly quiet town. The square stone or stuccoed houses were laid out in neat rows around a cen-

tral block of stores. There were trees and flowers everywhere; they were meticulously planted and cared for.
Nothing in the town seemed out of place; it was modern but
not at all fashionable, charming but not at all quaint. The
women in their neat cotton dresses, the shopkeepers in their
white aprons, the children in short pants or short dresses
playing docilely in the yards, were all sturdy and tidy and a
little sullen. They all said, *"Guten Tag,"* when we went by.

I asked a lot of questions, out of nervousness. I could see
that Frau König was beginning to tire of my anxious gaiety, as
well as of Käthe's stubborn refusal to talk. Frau König's forehead twisted more than ever. I could almost see the little
bubble of pain darting under the skin. Käthe noticed it too,
for suddenly, as we paused at a stop sign, she was asking her
mother if we could walk home from town.

"It's going to rain," warned Frau König, but she couldn't
help looking relieved.

"We won't be long," said Käthe. "I want to show Elizabeth something."

As soon as her mother's car had turned the corner Käthe
started walking me rapidly towards the hillside. "A short-
cut," she said.

"Is your mother all right?" I asked helplessly.

"Migraine."

"Oh, no wonder," I said. "And there I was, talking and
talking."

For the first time since we'd arrived Käthe smiled. "No,
she likes you. I can tell. She thinks you're a nice girl."

I waited a moment, then burst out, half in remorse, half in
anger, "I don't know what's wrong with me. Home was
never that great. My father has a girlfriend and my mother
drinks too much. They're always fighting. My brothers can't
wait to leave either. None of them care about me. They were
glad to see me go."

We had reached the top of the hill and stood panting with
exertion. It was cold and windy in the late afternoon; the
grass was turning a color I'd never seen before, a dark green,
with an iridescent undertone. For a moment, the light

seemed to shrink entirely out of the air and invest itself in the land, so that we appeared to be illuminated from below, as if each shard of grass were equipped with a tiny spotlight, a radiant point at the root that traveled up to meet us.

"I knew you were lying," Käthe said softly, as if it didn't matter. "The only way not to lie is to be silent, to think about other things."

"Why did you want to come?" I said. "It's so terrible."

I couldn't see her face clearly but I felt Käthe turn towards me, ungainly but solid above the carpet of illuminated green.

"You know," she said. "I wanted to see my brother."

"I thought you wanted to show me where you grew up, so I could understand."

"Maybe that a little too. Yes, maybe that most of all."

There was a sort of crackling in the air and then the light was drawn up out of the land again and flew across the sky. Lightning flashed a few miles away; in the seconds before the boom it was very silent.

"Look," said Käthe, pointing to a group of white buildings down in the valley on the other side of town. "That's the hospital where I stayed." Her voice was so calm that I didn't bother to ask why. When the great shuddering crash of thunder came, with the rain just behind it, we took off running, fast down the easy slope, and holding hands so we wouldn't fall.

———— • ————

"My therapist," said Nathalie, "spent all his time trying to persuade me that being a lesbian was sick. 'This is 1980,' I told him. 'No one believes that anymore.' I just wanted some help adjusting, figuring it all out. Finally I stopped going to him. I found a lesbian support group."

"I'd like to stop going too," said Clara. "I wish I had the courage to tell my father what I think of him to his face. He made a lot of money in the war, do you know what that means? How afterwards he felt and how he punished himself and us? When I remember my childhood. . . ."

"I don't know if it's worth it ever to go back and to re-experience anything," I said. "It can only be painful."

"Silence is painful too," said Clara softly, and Nathalie added, "We grew up knowing not to ask questions, being taught to forget what we had never learned. We want to remember now, even when it hurts."

———————•———————

The next day, Sunday, Käthe's brother Peter, the astrophysicist, arrived from Berlin. He wasn't at all what I'd expected. In his late twenties, tall and muscular, wearing light wool pants and a black turtleneck under a tight jacket of fawn suede, he looked like an Italian male model. Peter was richly, elegantly masculine, from his expensive boots to his fine Swiss watch, from his longish, carefully styled hair to his aviator glasses.

I stared rudely as he came breezing in, smoking a small cigar and carrying a leather satchel and camera case. No wonder Käthe resented him. It was obvious whom fortune had shined on in this family. Yet when I looked over at Käthe I found her to be overjoyed. She rushed to him, less like a duck than a puppy, wiggling up and down, inviting and shying from a hug. Käthe's shoulders shook, her bluegray eyes widened to ponds of love.

Peter took it easily. Cigar dangling from his lip like a tiny stick of dynamite, he slapped his sister on the back, shook his father's misshapen hand and hugged his mother with filial indifference. When we were introduced he gave me a charming and comprehensive smile, as if to say, "Families, aren't they ridiculous? But you and I understand each other."

Suddenly the bleak atmosphere of the house had changed. Frau König brought out Kirsch, Herr König offered Peter his chair and Käthe . . . Käthe, who I'd been positive held a deep and lasting grudge against her brother ... she was the most devoted of all. She took his satchel and hugged it unconsciously to her breast, she rushed to put the footstool under his sleek boots, she hung over his chair giggling laboriously, a fish gasping for air.

Peter patted her hand and looked at me. "Glad to see me, then?" Through his tinted glasses I could see that he was winking. I couldn't help winking back.

At first I told myself that I liked Peter because he spoke English to me. I hadn't realized how much I missed the sound of my language in the air and on my tongue. After having struggled sincerely and intensely for almost three months to speak German and only German, after having worked my way through the entire grammar book, through *Siddhartha* and *Tonio Kroger* and *Zarathustra*, after having had my pronunciation corrected daily by Käthe, I now—suddenly and overwhelmingly—gave in to the desire to speak English and only English.

Käthe, amazed and uncomprehending, could only stare as I unleashed a flood of previously unspoken thoughts and feelings. The relief of not having to choose between verbs nor grammatically construct my every small subtlety was enormous. I became, on the spot, instantly more relaxed; my jaw muscles loosened and my tongue quickened.

Not only did I find Peter a good conversationalist, I also thought him attractive, brilliant ... and kind. He had the lubricative kind of personality that went right to the trouble spot, the center of this family's creaky machinery, that oiled it and soothed it and made it run easily.

He was sympathetic to his mother, for instance, in asking her about the neighbors and the garden. Yet he also placed his hands on her twisting forehead one afternoon, smoothing out by gentle force the migraine pain. He talked to his father of politics and the economy, arguing without contradicting. The older man became quite talkative at meals now, brisk and opinionated.

Peter's friendliness towards me and his obvious concern

for Käthe made me ashamed I'd ever thought badly of him. Of course it hadn't been his fault that Käthe had had to leave school, or that she'd had to work in a shop. He'd only been eighteen or nineteen then, with a brilliant future before him. Should he have said no? It was only to his credit now that he still cared what happened to his sister. He asked her questions about Düsseldorf and her studies, chided her for not seeing more plays and films, gave her several books to read, and joked that her friendship with me had broadened her horizons: "Next you'll be traveling to America!" he told Käthe.

"No, seriously," he said to me, in his British-accented English, "you will be good for our little Katey. She doesn't go out enough."

I didn't tell him that neither Käthe nor I went out at all, preferring to spend our time in her room discussing the fine points of philosophy. By the second day of his visit I was trying hard to forget that I even knew Käthe. My entire energies were concentrated on making Peter like me.

I didn't know if Käthe realized the extent of my disaffection. I felt her sometimes staring at me, but I never responded. I answered half-heartedly when she addressed me, and made deliberate mistakes.

Peter laughed, "Look, Elizabeth is forgetting her German already."

I did notice, however, that the calm and quiet dignity Käthe had shown with her parents had vanished with Peter's arrival. I didn't blame it on him; I didn't know what to blame it on. I only knew that I had been on the verge of seeing her in a new light, the Nietzschean, sky-splitting light of that evening on the hill; and now all that was gone. Käthe was again the awkward, embarrassing acquaintance—I refused to call her friend—of the Mädchensheim. I couldn't believe that I'd gone around with her for almost two months, that I'd allowed myself to feel sympathy for her, that I'd tried to share my thoughts with her and that I had even begun to long, sometimes, for a greater closeness between us.

———•———

"I think my problem was going to a male therapist in the first place," said Nathalie, leaning back against Clara's knee and letting Clara run her fingers through her light and frisky hair. "Something happens when you're around a man, especially a professional. A desire to please, to impress. You're talking in his language, letting him set the rules. . . ."

"A woman counselor can affect you in the same way," Clara argued. "It depends on the person."

"I think I know what Nathalie's saying," I broke in. "Haven't we all betrayed a woman for a man sometime in our lives?"

"I don't think I'm saying that," said Nathalie.

"I think Elizabeth is," said Clara.

They looked at me with curiosity. I laughed, a little painfully. "Sometimes I wonder if we don't all treat the women's movement like a new religion. I mean, once you're converted, you're absolved of all previous sins. We're all so very righteous about our former lives. It wasn't our fault, *they* made us do it. And yet, all our actions had some effect. We were affected too, still are. Can you ever be forgiven, forgive yourself?"

Clara brought me within their circle. "Are you crying? Don't cry, Elizabeth."

Nathalie hugged us both. "Only, I wish I could speak English better. It's hard for me sometimes to understand, to say what I mean."

"It's hard for me, too," I said.

———•———

Peter lit my Attika cigarettes and smoked his tiny cigars. We sat up late, he and I and Käthe, after their parents had gone to bed, on lawnchairs in the neat backyard, watching the stars in the spring sky.

Peter talked, mostly in English, with hurried translations for his sister, about his work in Berlin, about his imminent departure for Peru. Eclipses were his specialty; he was going to the Andes to view one next month. He would visit Machu Picchu, climb the Inca Trail.

We all stared up at the sky. Käthe said something about the astronauts, the moon shot.

"The frontiers of knowledge are indeed opening up," Peter told her in German. "Incredible that in another month there will be men walking on the moon." He turned to me, with that blend of irony and interest I found so seductive and lit my cigarette. "You must be so excited, Elizabeth, knowing that it's your country about to make history."

"Oh yes," I said. I glanced at Käthe, glad she didn't understand my little burst of national pride. I had so carefully squelched any conversation about the Apollo flight with her.

Peter went on in German, "The amount of preparation, of scientific trial and error it's taken to achieve this feat is nothing short of astounding. Here we have three men, three ordinary men, blasting off from earth with enormous rocket power, then loosing the rockets and traveling up and onward in a small, a tiny capsule. . . ." He described each detail as if he personally had imagined the flight and had overseen it every step of the way. Yet there was something more disarming than arrogant in his description. In spite of the flood of very Germanic grandiloquence, Peter continued to look like an advertisement for elegant southern European men's wear. He was still wearing his blue-tinted aviator glasses. I wondered idly if he could really see the stars he was pointing to above. I wondered even more if he could see me. And I especially wondered how I could make him like me enough to make him want to see me again.

Then I glanced at Käthe. Her square face was rapt, almost exalted. By the look of her she was traveling up with the astronauts, letting go one rocket after another, soaring into the stratosphere.

Peter looked at her too and his tone immediately changed,

became easy, bantering. "Now Käthe here, what does she know about space? She broke that little telescope she used to have, didn't she?"

Käthe blinked, fell and burst into silent laughter, covering her mouth.

It was pitiful.

Peter took Käthe and me to the train station after dinner Monday night and while Käthe was buying a magazine and some chocolate, he said, "You have known my sister a long time now?"

"Six or eight weeks, that's all."

"How much has she told you about her life?"

"Well. . . ." I hesitated. It seemed an odd question. "I got the idea she was cheated out of going to school and had to go to work instead. I don't know how much I believe that anymore." I wished we could talk about something else. It was the first time we'd been alone together, even for an instant. I wanted him to ask for my address, to say he'd enjoyed meeting me, anything personal.

"Whatever happened," he said, "it was necessary."

"She said she forgave you," I remembered, but I didn't really understand what he was talking about.

"Did she? I don't know. I hope so, I forgive her." And for some reason he took off his aviator glasses. My impression of him changed immediately and unfavorably. His eyes were a weakish pale blue, his jaw overlarge without the balance of the wide frames. But the strangest thing was a white hairless scar on one temple, not a duelling scar, but a thick crescent of flesh near his eye. He looked like a bad Nazi from a war movie. I shivered automatically and said the first thing that came into my head.

"We're not really friends, you know, Käthe and I. It's just because we're at the Mädchensheim that we know each other."

That made Peter smile. He put his glasses back on and his voice resumed its playful tone; he was again the worldly Italian model. "Oh, you're too young for all of this. You can't be more than sixteen, can you?"

"I'm eighteen. I'm going to college soon."

He gave me a peck on the cheek as Käthe came up and then pressed her ungainly body to his elegant one for an instant. She clung to him. She said, "Visit me. Visit me. Visit me."

There was a note of hysteria in her voice that seemed to alarm him. He held her firmly at arm's length. "Good-bye, Käthe. I'll write you and see you when I come back. You must study and work hard. No dreaming. Elizabeth will keep an eye on you."

He winked at me from behind his sky-blue glasses as Käthe and I boarded the train.

Three

I didn't have a plan. I certainly didn't plan to walk inside the Mädchensheim. Yet I did. Two girls sitting at a table looked enquiringly at me. I stuttered, "Do you speak English?"

"*Nein.*"

I knew this room. I knew it all. There was the desk, the office. But so small.

I didn't really believe I could still speak German but I could. I said, "I am an American who lived here twelve years ago."

One of them stood up. "Let me get Frau Holtz."

She was still here. I hadn't counted on this. On seeing her again. She came down the corridor from her room, rubbing her hands together, staring at me. She was only a little older, a little bonier.

"I'm Elizabeth Michaels," I said. "I lived here twelve years ago. Worked here."

"American?"

"Yes."

"I don't remember." She shook her head. "I suppose you did."

———— • ————

Shortly after our trip to Käthe's parents', a new woman joined the staff of the Mädchensheim as an assistant to Frau Holtz. Fräulein Schmidt was slender and flat-chested, very tall and very brown-skinned, with a black mole the size of a dime at the corner of her mouth. Her shirts were crackling crisp and always tucked into belted dark pants, but her general air was less formal than alert and warm. She was almost too confidential, the sort of person who leaned on you when talking and fixed you with a sympathetic stare. Also, her breath was bad.

One by one, she arranged conferences with all the girls to talk about their problems and plans for the future. I was initially suspicious of Fräulein Schmidt and, when my appointment came around, grew defensive at the idea of explaining my literary aspirations, much less my now severe bouts of homesickness. But she listened gently, offered a few suggestions and, before I knew it, had me sitting in on an art history class at the Kunstakademie.

In spite of having resisted all Frau Holtz's efforts to make me more sociable, I fell in with this new scheme with something like relief. Through the class I started to meet some new people—an older woman painter from Brussels and a sculpture student named Hans. When he became my regular boyfriend, my status at the Mädchensheim went up considerably, and I forgot I'd ever considered the dental hygiene students unworthy of my company. I began to make friends with some of them, going out for a beer now and then or to a disco. I sat with them at mealtimes, and even Edeltrude and I found more to talk about. She redid my eyebrows and loaned me white knee socks, and one evening we went walking in the garden where she linked her arm through mine.

Both my reading and my writing sputtered out; I stopped memorizing Rilke and, when I took long strolls in the park now, it was with Hans to feed the ducks. I didn't ignore Käthe completely, but our torturous conversations about Nietzsche were a thing of the past. I became polite and friendly and after a week or two wasn't even making excuses not to see her. She accepted my changed attitude without asking any questions. Perhaps she even expected it. We never discussed the visit to her parents, my stories about my family, or how we had both acted with Peter. The evening I walked with Edeltrude in the garden I suddenly looked up at

Käthe's window and saw her watching us. I waved and, after a minute, she did too.

Part of the reason it was so easy not to see Käthe was that she was more and more taken up with Fräulein Schmidt. It began shortly after their scheduled conference and continued, with greater and greater intensity, all through June. You never saw them apart; either Käthe was hanging around the Fräulein's small office or the Fräulein was up in Käthe's room. You would have thought they'd known each other for years, the way they talked and laughed. It seemed to me that Käthe had found a much better friend than I had been; I was frankly relieved, and when the rumors started, was the first to deny them.

Gretchen said the Fräulein and Käthe hadn't come down to lunch one day, and when Eva had gone up to fetch them she'd discovered them holding hands.

That didn't worry me, but when I heard that Fräulein Schmidt and Käthe had been spotted in the Hofgarten with their arms around each other, I got nervous. I wanted to say I thought it was all right—German women were always linking arms, weren't they? How was I supposed to know when it was serious and when it wasn't?—but I was afraid of being laughed at, afraid the others would remember how much time Käthe and I had spent together back in the spring, afraid they would think she and I were. . . .

"*Lesbisch*," they whispered and giggled now at mealtimes, at the table, sneaking looks at the two of them. Stories of finding the Fräulein and Käthe in the shower together, in bed together, were circulated flagrantly. I began, in spite of myself, to believe them. I thought I understood now why Fräulein Schmidt's close, bad breath and sympathy made me uneasy. They were lesbians, with their short hair, sexless bodies and strong faces. Käthe had probably even been attracted to me. There was that time we'd held hands running down the hill, that time we'd stood close at the window. I shuddered to myself remembering and thought how lucky I was to have escaped. If Peter hadn't come for a visit I might still be Käthe's friend.

That the scandal didn't blow up was due to its being by now the end of June. Finished with their term at the dental hygiene school, the girls departed one by one for their homes in Stuttgart, Bonn, Cologne. I exchanged tearful farewells with several and promised to visit when I could. I was already planning my own vacation—a trip to Munich and Switzerland—before I returned home to begin the fall quarter. My parents had sent me two hundred dollars and told me to stay away as long as I liked.

By July most of the girls were gone. Both Frau Kosak and one of the cooks went on vacation too. Frau Holtz left for two weeks in France. Only a few, including me and Käthe and Fräulein Schmidt, stayed on. There was a ghostly quality to the Mädchensheim now, an almost secretive quiet that hovered in the halls and nearly empty dining room and that made me want to be outside as much as possible, in spite of the fact that it was very warm that summer. The streets were like cookie tins and even the tree-shaded park was drenched in humidity and lassitude. I spent most of my time with Hans in the deserted studios of the art school, helping him fire his clay figures. A few times I stayed the night with him and no one noticed. But in early July he left too and I was back on my own.

It was then that I began to feel jealous of Käthe and Fräulein Schmidt, just as the summer was reaching a point of unbearable heat and splendor. I couldn't remember any longer why I had ever disliked either of them, why I had thought them ugly—Fräulein Schmidt so crisp and warm, with her mole like a tiny black moon, and Käthe with her big, earnest bluegray eyes. Seeing the two of them together, happily chatting in the office, or working in the garden, I started to feel left out, to feel, furthermore, that I had never appreciated Käthe.

What had happened between us, anyway? I couldn't remember. We certainly had never fought about anything. No, all I recalled now were those rainy spring afternoons when we'd trudged through the streets arguing about *Heimweh*, or those cozy evenings in her room drinking tea and reading philosophy.

I began to write poetry again and it was full of bitterness, lost affection, melancholy. I took out my old copy of Nietzsche and sighed over it. I bought the *Herald Tribune* and read about the approaching moon shot. I started smoking seriously, a pack a day. I wrote letters to my parents that I didn't send, asking them why we all lied so much. I said it would serve them right if I stayed over here forever, that they didn't have any idea of how much I missed them.

One morning Fräulein Schmidt found me standing in a corner of the garden, at a loss to know what to do with myself. She walked quickly towards me, smiling, wearing one of her stiff shirts, unwrinkled in spite of the heat.

"So, Elizabeth," she addressed me without preliminary. "Your friends are all gone now, what do you do with yourself?"

"Nothing," I muttered.

"Lonely then? Homesick?"

The garden was a well of green, damp and sunflecked. I looked at her cheerful, strong face and wanted to cry, *Nobody understands me.*

"You must spend more time with me and Käthe then," Fräulein Schmidt urged. "We've had some delightful picnics in the country. Please come with us sometime."

I did cry then. I sobbed and sobbed, urgently at first, then comfortably, burying my face in her crisp shirt front. She smelled of pine soap, a little of bad breath. The last woman I had hugged had been my mother at the airport; underneath the Jean Naté fragrance she always wore had been the scent of buoyant good-bye cocktails.

"When are you going?" I finally asked.

Fräulein Schmidt laughed and held me out at arm's length while she applied a handkerchief poultice to my tears. The black mole danced on her lip.

In less than an hour Käthe and I were packed into Fräulein Schmidt's Volkswagen with a basket of food and headed out of the city. It was a brilliant day, hot but fresh, with white clouds twining themselves around the sun from time to time like airy cats around a fat yellow cushion. I can't remember what we talked about in the car. I was so completely grateful to Fräulein Schmidt for taking me along, to Käthe for acting as if I had never stopped being her friend.

Yet I remember that afternoon, in fits and starts, very well. Partly because I was the happiest I'd been for many weeks, and partly because, after it, nothing was the same. We drove about twenty miles out into the countryside, past an historic castle and several small towns. We stopped at none of them, however, and instead Fräulein Schmidt—who was now urging me to call her Monika—pulled up near a wooded stream.

"Swim first and then eat," she suggested. But although the day was hot, the water was chill and bubbling. We contented ourselves with rolling our pants legs up and wading back and forth, building dams and skipping rocks. Monika was the ringleader. I still recall her firm brownish calves, the water reflecting up on them, making rainbows through the dark hair. Käthe was awkward and fell in twice, but she only laughed and took off her shirt to dry in the sun. We all took off our shirts then, and sat down to eat. It didn't seem strange to me, perhaps because the two of them were so casual.

We ate fresh cheese with pumpernickel and pears and hard, fatty sausage and drank beer. The beer made me sleepy under the sun. Whenever I opened my eyes I saw Käthe's white skin and Monika's brown nipples, but soon I kept them closed, feeling only the grass sweet and soft under my cheek. And I thought, before drifting off, "The important thing is not to lie, ever. But is silence the only way?"

It didn't even make sense to me at the time.

When I woke up the two of them had their shirts back on and were discussing the Apollo flight, due to begin that evening.

Monika said, "Whenever I think of men on the moon I get a picture in my head. Of bugs beating senselessly against a light bulb. Buzz. Buzz. And then they burn up."

"Do you think they'll die there then?" I asked.

"Perhaps. The moon is a woman, you know, in every language but German. Maybe she'll grow angry when they try
to land, maybe she'll burn them up with her light."

"I always think of the moon as a terrible cold place," I
said. "Like a dusty bathtub in a deserted house."

Käthe said dreamily, "I would like to go there someday.
Perhaps I have already been. Sometimes it all seems so familiar to me. How you could walk like a feather on the surface,
so light you hardly touched. Sometimes I think I may have
done that."

"In a dream?" I asked.

"No, in my life."

I giggled, suddenly thinking of the mannequins in the
show windows along the Königsallee, flying through the air,
silver stick figures. "Oh, Käthe, you're just crazy." I reached
out and touched her arm. I felt closer to her than I had in
weeks.

There was a short, constrained silence, then Käthe
laughed, in the old way, hysterically but silently, with her
hand pressed to her mouth, and Monika reproved me, "Please
don't say things like that."

"It's an American expression," I floundered. Idiomatic-
ally, I supposed, my German still left something to be
desired.

Yet we had a wonderful time on the way home. I asked
Käthe whether, now she'd finished the dental hygiene
course, she'd stay on in Düsseldorf and get a job.

"But we haven't told you!" said Monika. Her hair was
damp from the heat and her forehead glistened. More earthy
now than crisp, she was driving with the window down, at
high speed. "Käthe, tell her. We are going traveling. We want
to go to South America and do something there. We don't
know what, something interesting."

I wasn't prepared for this, but was able to quickly endorse
the idea. "But won't it be awfully expensive?"

"Oh, I have lots of money," Monika said, and her black

mole sat on her smile like a licorice drop. "And Käthe will go to the University there."

"In South America?"

Käthe smiled, enjoying Monika's enthusiasm. She was rolling her window up and down absentmindedly. "I don't expect much," she said strangely.

Monika chided her. "Oh, it will be wonderful. We'll start completely over. I promise you that."

It didn't occur to me to ask why they would need to. "Well, if I'm ever in Argentina, I'll look you up."

"Peru," said Käthe. "Peter says Peru is beautiful. You can see the sky better than anywhere from there."

"Peter won't be there then," Monika reminded her, passing a car with dangerous speed. Then she leaned out the window and waved back at the car. The hot wind blew her short hair flat on her head. "Will he?" she asked.

"No, I suppose not," said Käthe.

———•———

"You're not calling yourself a lesbian yet?" asked Nathalie one evening while we sat together in her room drinking Moselle.

"Well, I've only just started, you know, being attracted to women."

"Oh, I doubt that," she laughed.

"If I could just fall in love, it would be easier."

"You seem to me the lonely type," she noted. "Like Clara."

"It's not just that," I said, and then, abruptly, "Do you ever feel afraid?"

I was thinking of my first real sexual affair with a woman, last year. Before that, a sister among feminist sisters, I used to be able to hug and kiss women friends in public without a qualm. After I got involved with Lucy I was far more nervous, wondering what her neighbors and my own would think, what my family and co-workers would say, how my "sisters" would react. As it turned out, it had all been over within a month anyway, and hardly anybody knew.

"Not so afraid," said Nathalie, shaking her lively hair. "But if I ever break up with Agatha I may be. I was like you before, wondering, and then—I met her and *knew*. But I don't have too much experience finding women like I used to find men. And sometimes I feel there are so few of us, us lesbians. It's isolating."

"Much better than the old days."

"And still, still so much the same." She drank more wine and brought out a book. "Now look at this." It was about the women's clubs in Berlin in the twenties. The *Damenklubs*. "They came from everywhere: England, America, Scandinavia, France, Germany of course; they had such a strong culture of their own. Books, journals, music and cabaret and theater, even a film, *Mädchen in Uniform*. Look at these photos, how they dressed, their faces. I wish I'd known *that* one, she's so nice-looking. . . ."

"What happened to those clubs, those women?"

"You know," Nathalie said. Her bright face shut down for an instant. "They were killed or they pretended or they left the country."

I thought of a book I'd read about the Pink Triangle, the homosexual equivalent of the yellow star the Jews were made to wear. Naturally the book concentrated on the men, lesbians invisible, not taken seriously, as always. But if that meant more of them had survived? *Had* more survived? And what had it meant to survive by becoming invisible?

"I think I am a lesbian," I told Nathalie.

"Now are you sure? Don't make a mistake!" she teased and then more seriously, with a hug. "It doesn't matter to me what you or Clara call yourself. It's not so important."

"But isn't it?" I said, trying to imagine myself in Berlin fifty years ago, hanging out in the *Damenklubs* while it was fun and disappearing when it wasn't. "If they started taking gay people away again, what would you do? What would any of us say we were?"

"Not this time," Nathalie said, putting her arm firmly

around my shoulder. "No, not this time. We'll fight. We're fighting already. Can't you feel that?" Her voice shook a little but she held me playfully. "I'm doing judo, after all, and I'm not going to be taken anywhere I don't want to go."

———————•———————

We were in Frau Holtz's sitting room, just off the foyer, watching the take-off from Cape Kennedy that evening, when the door to the Mädchensheim sounded with a disconcerting ring. Nobody wanted to answer it; it was the countdown.

"I suppose I should go," said Monika.

The bell rang again, twice, insistent.

The rockets flared white on the screen, filled its small square with roiling plumage. The German announcer's voice shot up too, less practiced than convulsive. The Apollo team had made it. They had left the earth. They were gone.

Käthe got up and went into the foyer to answer the door. Almost immediately we heard her cry, "Peter!"

Monika gave me a startled look. I thought, am I really going to see him again? Monika stood, pulled back her shoulders; the black mole went up like a battle flag. Very deliberately she took me by the hand and led me into the foyer.

"Elizabeth," said Peter, continuing in English. "How very charming to see you again."

"Yes," I goggled. He was handsome as ever and beautifully dressed in tassled leather boots and a Peruvian embroidered shirt open on his chest. His aviator glasses wrapped around his lean face like a semi-transparent blue bandage.

"Fräulein Schmidt," said Monika, holding out her hand.

"Ah, a new director?"

"A new assistant. Frau Holtz is away on a trip. She will be back tomorrow."

"*Ach so*," Peter nodded, turning to Käthe. "Go on, get your coat, Katchen. You want to hear all about my trip, don't you?"

Käthe, without another word, rushed upstairs. Peter watched her go, smiling faintly.

"She's already eaten, we all ate early so we could watch the moon shot. . . ," Monika began with a kind of desperately controlled politeness, but Peter interrupted her, clapping his hand to his styled hair, though not enough to derange it.

"It's happened already? I thought it was later tonight."

"It was wonderful," I said, rather stupidly. "You would have liked it."

"Dear little Elizabeth, our little American friend. You saw this important historical event then. Don't you feel proud?"

"You just missed it," said Monika, "not five minutes ago." She seemed slightly more sure of herself. The sight of Peter's elegance must have amazed her just as it had me. Soon, I thought, she'll realize how kind and sympathetic and brilliant he really is.

Monika went on, "It will be on the news again. If you and Käthe care to stay I can make coffee. We have a torte as well."

I held my breath, hoping he would say yes.

"You could tell us all about Peru," Monika continued, now smiling in her warm, confidential way. "I'm sure Elizabeth would love to hear about your travels."

"I would. I'd just love it."

Käthe came barreling back down the stairs with a sweater and her purse, face alight. She hardly looked at me or Monika. "I'm ready."

"Why don't I take you all out?" suggested Peter. "We can come back here later and watch the news."

"An excellent idea," said Monika. "I have a favorite spot."

"So have I," said Peter.

It was a beautiful evening, clear and balmy as California. The streets were crowded, the shop windows and signs had never glittered more brightly, the canal was a river of light crisscrossed by shadowbridges. We went everywhere, we went to half a dozen places I had never been before. It should have been one of the high spots of my entire stay in Germany. I didn't know why I wasn't enjoying myself very much.

I kept feeling left out somehow, even though Peter occasionally took my arm when we crossed a street, even though Monika bent her head to talk to me from time to time. I might not have been there, for all that Käthe noticed me, but the other two bothered me more than she did. It wasn't fair that I couldn't speak German as well as Monika, that I couldn't seem to hold Peter's interest the way she could. I knew I was a much more fascinating person. He'd seemed to understand that once, now he was only curious about Monika. He wanted to know all about her, where she'd grown up, what she'd studied in school, what she wanted to do in life.

He said she looked familiar to him. She said, "I have that sort of face." She said she'd spent most of her adult life in Denmark. She'd taught German. She expected to go back there eventually. She made a joke about the Germans being too repressive.

I expected that Monika would tell him all about the trip to South America, or that Käthe would. I didn't think anyone would mind then, if I brought it up. I added that I hoped to visit the two of them sometimes.

We were by then in an expensive little restaurant in the Altstadt. It was Peter's favorite place. I could see how he would like it. It was modish and restrained, more French than German, with white linen tablecloths and fine china. There were lanterns at every table, round and plump and of blue glass, so that the candles flickering inside them gave off a pale cool glow, like the color of Käthe's eyes sometimes, a light lunar blue.

"What's this?" asked Peter, staring at his sister. "You're going to Peru?" He didn't seem angry, only amused, ironic, like the time he asked Käthe, "What do you know about space?"

"Just an idea," said Monika, before Käthe could answer.

Käthe started to laugh, then caught herself. But her face still twitched nervously, with guilt and fear and even anger. "You went," she said. "Why can't I?"

"Oh, I have nothing against it," he said, lighting a tiny cigar from the lantern. "But all the same, two girls traveling alone in South America, it's ridiculous. You don't know what it's like there."

"It's true we're not famous physicists," said Monika testily. Her mole was quivering on her upper lip like a dying fly. I watched it, fascinated, suddenly beginning to understand that she hated and feared Käthe's brother. Yet I felt helpless to do anything. It was the same when my mother and father fought, neither of them raising their voices, but still managing to put furious anger into their words. I always wanted to stop them, but when I tried, they said, "But we weren't fighting, dear."

"What was it like there, Peter?" I asked desperately in English. "Did you see the eclipse? Was it a good one? I saw an eclipse once, my mother and father took me to see it. We went to Griffith Observatory, that's in Los Angeles. It was the only eclipse I ever saw, but I was so young I didn't really understand it. It got so dark and cold suddenly, like a nightmare, and no one said anything. I couldn't understand what had happened to the moon, where it went. My father told me it didn't go anywhere, but I didn't believe him. Make it come back, Daddy, I said. Make it come back."

My hands were shaking. I tried to laugh sophisticatedly. "Isn't that absurd? 'Make it come back!'"

"This was an eclipse of the sun," answered Peter in German, coldly. "We gathered a great deal of important information."

Then I, too, felt frightened of him.

FOUR

"Would you like to look around a bit?" Frau Holtz asked.

I numbly nodded, followed her upstairs. Everything was the same, down to the plants in the windowsills. I recalled that I used to water them.

"Elizabeth Michaels?" she mused. "Do you remember your room?"

I led the way.

"Who was your roommate?"

"Edeltrude."

"From Bad Ems?"

"Bad Godesberg, I think."

"Hmmm."

She opened the door to someone's room, the one Edeltrude and I used to share.

"Only one girl to a room now," Frau Holtz said.

Even one to a room it looked tight. No wonder Edeltrude and I hadn't gotten along.

Frau Holtz gave me a good look. I became acutely conscious that I was wearing one gold hoop and one pearl stud in my ears.

"And what do you do now?" she asked.

"I'm a writer." I wanted less for her to be impressed than for her to recognize that I had grown up.

"I'm sorry I don't remember you," she sighed.

We were passing the corridor off of which Käthe had had her room, when Frau Holtz suddenly asked, "And who were your friends?"

"I only had one," I told her. "Käthe König."

"The girl whose brother was the doctor?"
"No. The girl who killed herself."
"Yes, that's the one."

———————•———————

That evening with Peter must have been the day before
Frau Holtz came back because the next thing I remember
was her asking me to come down to her office. I went, if not
willingly, then with no real apprehensions. The worst I could
imagine was that she might reprimand me for not doing my
work during her absence. My thoughts centered especially
on the unwashed upstairs hall and I wasn't at all prepared to
hear her say:
    "I received a telephone call from Fräulein König's brother
this morning."
    I waited, puzzled.
    "He told me some disturbing things about Fräulein König
and Fräulein . . . Schmidt."
    The French sun had tanned Frau Holtz's corrugated skin
to the color of an overripe banana peel. Somehow she no
longer looked so placidly maternal to me, but almost coldly
militant, gathering up the reins of her authority like a general
who'd been on leave.
    "Such things do not happen in the Mädchensheim. I will
not allow them."
    "What things?" I finally managed.
    Frau Holtz's yellow-brown skin began to blotch violet
around her ears and neck; she grew pinched and dry about
the lips. "I want you to tell me what you've seen while I've
been gone."
    "I'm hardly ever here."
    Frau Holtz made an effort, and the violet gradually dis-
appeared from the banana. She coughed and began again in a
gentler voice, "Fräulein König's brother is very concerned
about her friendships. As one who has been primarily
responsible for her here in Düsseldorf, naturally I am also

concerned. It has been a source of satisfaction to me that Käthe, Fräulein König, has done so much better while she has been at the Mädchensheim."

"But she didn't do better," I blurted out unwisely, "until. . . ."

"Until Fräulein Schmidt came, you mean?"

"You don't understand," I said. "For the first time in her life she's been happy."

"Elizabeth," said Frau Holtz firmly, severely compassionate now. "I am not accusing you of anything, if that's what you think. You are a simple young American girl. You were lonely and had not many friends. . . ."

Suddenly a terror arose in me that she *was* accusing me, that she did suspect me of something. "What are you talking about?"

"I am talking about Käthe König, a girl who has a history of mental problems and abnormal . . . fixations. I am talking about a girl who spent some years in a hospital for treatment. I am talking about a girl who tried to kill her brother when he intervened. I am also talking about a woman who lied about her qualifications and her background in order to become my assistant."

I couldn't take it in. I couldn't seem to understand why Frau Holtz was so angry. "But what have we done?" I wailed, for the first time implicating myself along with Monika and Käthe.

Frau Holtz shook her head. "You're not helping me, Elizabeth."

"But what have we *done*?"

Frau Holtz suddenly looked discouraged. "If it's true you've done nothing you needn't worry. But Fräulein Schmidt must leave today. As for Käthe, her brother is coming to get her tomorrow."

———— • ————

Clara invited me to share her bed one night. "So we can

talk.''

She told me that if it had been hard for Nathalie to tell her that she'd become a lesbian, it was hard for her too. ''She was my best friend, then suddenly I felt . . . overrun, is that the word?''

''Superseded maybe . . . but are you sure? Lesbians need best friends too.''

''But maybe only other lesbians. Did she tell you I may move out?''

''No. Why?''

''Oh, Elizabeth, I think I'm jealous.''

We held each other and I felt my attraction to her turning hot and sweet.

''I wish I could,'' Clara murmured, ''I wish I could. I wish I had more love in me, not so much fear and hate.''

''What are you so afraid of?'' I said, kissing her cheek, her forehead, stopping myself. ''Don't be afraid, don't let them make you afraid.''

''It doesn't come from them,'' she cried. ''It comes from me.''

''It comes from them,'' I said.

———— • ————

I didn't see Monika go and I didn't seek out Käthe. I spent the day out of the Mädchensheim, walking through the streets of Düsseldorf. I remember it was very hot, without a breath of air to leaven the heavy stone sidewalks, the weighted buildings. I wondered why I had ever come to this city, out of all the places in the universe. It still seemed foreign to me, worse than foreign, unfamiliar.

In the Hofgarten the red clay of the paths burned like fire against the too-green grass; the sky bristled angrily with heat. A blue sky, turning black and violet. A thunderstorm was coming. I could feel it building in the prickly air, like a series of sobs in my throat, choking me.

Käthe was not crazy, I should never have used that word.

There was a difference between insanity and fear. I had seen my father bring his hands down on the white and black keys of my mother's piano; I had heard my mother clinking ice in a glass at midnight, waiting for my father to come home. These things frightened me; they were not insane. In between there were picnics and trips to the beaches, there was my mother sewing in the kitchen and my father reading us parts of the newspaper.

I had wanted to get away from them so badly.

I sat on a bench in the park, smoking cigarette after cigarette, and tried to imagine myself far out in space, alongside the astronauts looking down. Only when I did that, looked down from a place near the bitter cold moon, all I could see was myself, a tiny stick figure, full of *Heimweh* for nothing and nobody real, poking out from a round, hot, blue and green ball, like a marble, a marble spinning in blackness, spinning and spinning.

When the thunderstorm came I stood by a tree. I saw the earth and sky separate, expand with a bolt of lightning, contract with a charge of rain. Everything was purple and red and green, like a wound being washed clean. I was glad, then, that I had never loved anybody much, that I was beginning to be old enough to be free. I would never go home to my parents' again. I would stay here or go somewhere else, a rainy place. I would have a little room by myself, read poetry and write. I would learn to write what mattered, draw a line around craziness and keep it out. That wouldn't be lying, it would only be silence sometimes. And in the evening I would go out into the streets and look at the moon, raining or not. It would always be there, cold and white and distant, less like a memory than a stone marker in the night.

It wasn't me who found her, though it could have been, but Anneliese, the witch of the cellar. She came screaming up into our breakfast the next morning and no one could understand what she said. Finally the cook went downstairs to see what had frightened Anneliese so, and she in turn came shrieking up.

She had seen Käthe hanging, she had seen Käthe dead. She said it was a sight she would never forget.

———————•———————

"Clara, Nathalie," I said. "I don't know what you'll think of me when I tell you this. . . . I have been to Germany before. I lived here once. There were things that happened. . . . I didn't come to visit you intending to relive any of it, but it's so close now, it's all so close. . . ."

Clara came into the bathroom. "Nathalie. . . . Oh," she said, seeing me at the mirror. "I thought it was Nathalie in here. I thought I heard German."

Nathalie came in behind her, sat on the toilet sleepily. "What shall we do tomorrow? It's Saturday."

"*Ich muss nach Düsseldorf fahren.* I have to go to Düsseldorf," I added in case they hadn't understood.

"I told you," said Nathalie to Clara. "There was something."

"Do you want company?" said Clara, touching my arm.

"No, I mean—when I come back. . . ."

"We'll be here."

———————•———————

Peter came immediately. I didn't see Monika until some days after the funeral. Peter made all the arrangements and wept at the funeral, taking off his aviator glasses so that the crescent scar shone smooth and white. Monika didn't even go to the funeral. Peter gave me Käthe's much-marked Nietzsche collection; he said his sister was a bright girl who could have led a normal life eventually. Monika made a reservation for Buenos Aires. Peter said he hoped Käthe had finally found peace. Monika said Peter would have to live with this his whole life long.

Peter took me out for coffee and confided the story of

Käthe's mental illness.

"We were very close as children, but even then I could see that in spite of her intelligence there was something not quite right with her. She was awkward and plain, slow in school; she didn't have any friends. She depended quite a lot on me. At first I didn't mind, it was flattering to have her reading the same books, trying to study what I studied. That's where her obsessions with Nietzsche began. I was very fond of Nietzsche as a boy. But then I went away to school, to the University. . . .

"Käthe always needed someone. She formed a romantic attachment to one of her teachers. It was reciprocated. Of course that couldn't be allowed. You know our small town. There was talk. The only thing to do was to take Käthe out of school. The teacher was dismissed. I took care of all that. . . . Käthe used to write me letters full of Nietzsche. When I began my course on astronomy she saved up money and bought a telescope, a pitiful little thing. You could barely see the moon in it. She sometimes stayed up all night watching the stars. I think it began to affect her mind. She talked of flying, of being two people, one above looking down. She said she was always watching herself to make sure she didn't make any mistakes. My parents couldn't handle her, they were afraid she might hurt herself. Fortunately there was an excellent treatment center not far from us, in the valley. Käthe spent five years there. She came out quieter, except for that nervous laugh. We thought she was completely cured. I suppose no one can ever be completely cured. . . ."

Peter looked pensively at his coffee. A small cigar was between his elegant fingers; he rolled it back and forth a few times before striking a match to it.

"But she tried to kill you," I said.

"It was an accident, I'm sure of it. She didn't know what she was doing. Sometimes I've doubted that she remembered it. . . . For the last few years we've been, we were closer than ever. I did all I could for her. I got her into the dental hygiene school. She was really a very bright girl, in her way, she could have had a normal life eventually."

I went to see Monika in her new room to tell her I was leaving sooner than I'd thought for Munich. That's when I found out she was leaving too. She hadn't even bothered to unpack when she'd moved from the Mädchensheim. Everything was in boxes and suitcases and she was wearing an unironed shirt. There were dark circles under her eyes; her mole looked dried out as a raisin from the force of her bad breath. She frightened me as much as she attracted me.

"I changed my name. I went away to England for a while after it all happened, then to Denmark," she said. "I never expected to see Käthe again. At first I hardly recognized her. She was much different when she was younger, when she was my student. She had a clear, fresh mind, the sort of mind a teacher hopes and longs to find. She was terribly honest, she never lied about anything. I suppose that was a clue right there to what was to happen. *Mein Gott*, you've seen her parents, and Peter. What use did they have for someone like her? And yet they couldn't leave her alone. She idolized her brother. She didn't understand that she got nothing back from him, that he took everything from her. She could have gone on to the University. She wanted to study philosophy. But everything was for him, for Peter. Her parents wanted to take her out of school. That's when it all came out, about her and me. Käthe could never keep anything back. You understand, it was not a sexual thing, not yet."

Monika watched me light another cigarette. A touch of the teacher was in her voice as she murmured, "That's bad for you, Elizabeth, to smoke so heavily at your age." Then she went on:

"I wasn't sure if he recognized me until Frau Holtz called me in and told me she knew my real name. But I didn't mean any harm. I would never have taken the job at the Mädchensheim if I'd known she was going to be there, Käthe. A student of dental hygiene, what could be more depressing? She never blamed her brother, she was so guilty about having tried to kill him that she loved him even more. More than me, more than herself. I know she was never crazy, or if she was, that he made her, her parents made her that way. I should never have abandoned her then. I thought I was doing the right thing, no . . . I was afraid for my reputation. Peter threatened to tell the school, to make it impossible for me to work again. And Käthe was so young. It was impossible."

Monika stared at me, almost angrily. "But what do you know about this? You never really knew Käthe, how could you understand her? You were not a good friend to her."

"That's not true. I mean, she got on my nerves some-times, the way she laughed and everything, but I always find something about a person I don't like, I mean. . . ."

"*I* could have helped her, she trusted me. If we had gone away as we planned, if you hadn't mentioned Peru. No, it wasn't your fault, I'm sorry. Peter was her guardian. I know now since he claimed the body. We would have had to deal with him. But I should have killed him for her this time. I should have been courageous instead of so afraid. Instead of letting her turn it against herself. I won't see her again.

"This time I won't see her again."

———•———

Frau Holtz took me down to the kitchen. It was just mid-day and the meal was almost finished. She said doubtfully to the cook, "Here is a girl from America who worked here many years ago. I don't suppose you remember her."

I didn't remember the cook at all, though I recalled every expression and gesture of Frau Holtz's.

"*Ja,*" said the cook simply, glancing at me as if it were a few weeks, instead of twelve years that had passed. "*Die kleine Elizabeth, sie weinte so viel und hatte so viel Heimweh.*" The little Elizabeth, who cried so much and was so homesick.

I laughed awkwardly. "Yes, that was me."

"You won't stay to lunch," invited Frau Holtz.
"No, thank you. But thank you. I'm sorry."
"I wonder why I can't remember you," she said. And seemed truly puzzled.

"It's safer to be invisible," I answered. But perhaps I didn't say it correctly, for Frau Holtz just smiled, shook my hand and showed me the door. My whole visit had taken just under fifteen minutes.

I stood in the garden a few moments longer, exhausted, and to give myself an excuse, took a picture of the Mädchens-heim. I began to wonder why I hadn't asked after Käthe's family. What had happened to Peter? And to Monika? And why hadn't I explained or disputed anything? Even Frau Holtz's one memory that Käthe's brother had been a doctor instead of a physicist.

Yet not for worlds would I have gone inside again.

The little Elizabeth, who cried so much and was so home-sick.

————•————

Early the morning after Käthe's funeral the astronauts started walking on the moon. It was three or four o'clock in the morning and the cook woke me up to come down and see the great event on television. I sat with her and two other girls, Heidi and Eva, in the gloomy dining room, watching the ghostly shadows take their first steps. I didn't want to be impressed and I wasn't—still, it almost hurt to hear their far-away American voices describing the marvels that they saw, the marvels that to us were only shivering gray and white images on a small screen.

I wished that Käthe could have been there, to see that they were not *Übermenschen*, but tiny, almost weightless fig-ures bouncing back and forth in their bulky suits, trying to get a toehold on the shifting surface, completely dependent on the fragile support systems that linked them to this earth. They were brave, I could have told Käthe, but at the same time there was something wrong with them, with the picture that flickered so strangely on the screen.

The way they talked, a jumble of code words and boyish

delight. Pleased with themselves, yet detached in tinny, lingering voices. As disconnected from each other as from the control center, the earth with its countries, cities, friends and family. My stomach started to ache, it was the homesickness and the sadness beginning again.

It was the fear I had watching the astronauts walking on the moon that they wouldn't get back alive. And that I, too, after having been through space and time to walk another surface than my own, would not return to tell the story of what I'd seen.

———————•———————

I had planned to stay in Düsseldorf a few hours. I glanced at my watch after leaving the Mädchensheim; it had only been forty minutes since the train pulled into the Hauptbahnhof. There was time enough to stroll around the city again, the city I had once known so well.

I turned right down a street of shops and walked a few blocks to the Hofgarten's far end. In the canal were ducklings, this spring as always.

I was lightheaded and speedy, as if I'd just drunk a cup of strong coffee. How could Frau Holtz not have remembered me? Had Edeltrude really been from Bad Ems? Had Peter really been a doctor? I had never tried to remember before.

After I left Düsseldorf that summer I traveled for two blank weeks in the Alps, then returned home to San Diego. I never went back to live with my parents, who, in any case, divorced shortly afterwards. My brothers stayed with my father and my mother went back to school. She and I became good friends about a year ago.

I, meanwhile, moved north to finish my degree in another state. I worked, I wrote, I lived with a man and then alone. I became a feminist, an activist; I wanted now to become a lesbian.

I had never told anyone about Käthe. I'd never thought of her from the day I left the Mädchensheim, twelve years ago.

Now, passing slowly through the Hofgarten, on paths my feet remembered better than my mind, I began to feel that I was walking somewhere, for some reason, that I was even in Düsseldorf for some reason, in Germany. And yet, I was also very sure that if I hadn't met Clara and Nathalie that day in Stanley Park, I wouldn't be here. I would never have come back.

I had survived. That had been enough until now.

I came to the other side of the Hofgarten, crossed under the busy street to the Altstadt. The first thing I saw when I turned the corner were the four statues, the four Muses in two pairs.

On the pedestal of one pair someone had scrawled a feminist slogan in red paint.

I thought that Nathalie and Clara would like this scene. I took out my camera. Tears ran down my face.

All unconcerned a group of three young women students was sitting at a bench to one side. They looked up casually to see me photograph the marble women.

One pair holding hands. One pair with their arms around each other.

Barbara Wilson's most recently published books include two feminist murder mysteries, *Sisters of the Road* and *Murder in the Collective*, and a novel, *Ambitious Women*. She has also translated *Cora Sandel: Selected Short Stories* from Norwegian and is working on another translation, *Nothing Happened*, a novel by Ebba Hasland. She is co-founder of Seal Press, where she works as an editor.

Typeset in 11-point Garth Graphic by John D. Berry at The Franklin Press. Printed on 60 lb. Simpson Opaque at Workshop Printers.

Other selected titles from Seal Press:

Fiction & Women's Studies

Girls, Visions and Everything
by Sarah Schulman
$8.95

Murder in the Collective
by Barbara Wilson
$7.95

Ambitious Women
by Barbara Wilson
$7.95

The Things That Divide Us
edited by Faith Conlon, Rachel da Silva and Barbara Wilson
$7.95

Every Mother's Son: The Role of Mothers in the Making of Men
by Judith Arcana
$10.95

Women in Translation

Two Women in One
by Nawal el-Saadawi
translated by Osman Nusairi and Jana Gough
$7.95 pb. $14.95 cl.

Egalia's Daughters
by Gerd Brantenberg
translated by Louis Mackay
$8.95 pb. $16.95 cl.

Cora Sandel: Selected Short Stories
translated by Barbara Wilson
$8.95 pb. $16.95 cl.

Early Spring
by Tove Ditlevsen
translated by Tiina Nunnally
$8.95 pb. $16.95 cl.

An Everyday Story: Norwegian Women's Fiction
edited by Katherine Hanson
$8.95 pb. $16.95 cl.